# The Seeds
of Happiness

*Translated from the French*
*Original title:* LES SEMENCES DU BONHEUR

Prosveta S.A – B.P.12 – 83601 Fréjus CEDEX (France)

ISSN 0763-2738
ISBN 2-85566-522-1
original edition: ISBN 2-85566-482-9

# Omraam Mikhaël Aïvanhov

# The Seeds of Happiness

*3rd edition*

**Izvor Collection — No. 231**

# PROSVETA

# TABLE OF CONTENTS

*Readers are asked to note that Omraam Mikhaël Aïvanhov's teaching was exclusively oral. This volume includes passages from several different lectures all dealing with the same theme.*

Chapter One

# HAPPINESS: A GIFT TO BE CULTIVATED

Human beings come into the world with certain aspirations; they need to love and be loved; they need to know, and they need to create. And it is the fulfilment of these aspirations that they call happiness. Before they can fulfil their aspirations, however, they need to add something more to the baggage they bring with them, for it is not enough to want something in order to obtain it. They want to love and be loved, but they find themselves alone and disappointed. They want to understand everything, and they understand very little and are continually confused and disorientated. They want to create, and they manage to produce only monstrosities. In order to achieve all their aspirations, they are going to have to complete a long apprenticeship under an instructor who is qualified to lead them on the path of true love, true understanding and true creation.

All human beings want happiness, but they don't know how to go about it. They don't even know that there is work to be done and a discipline to be observed in order to obtain it. They think that just because they are here on earth, they only need to eat, drink, sleep, earn a living and bring children into the world, and they should automatically be happy. But animals do pretty much the same things, so what is the difference? To be on earth is no guarantee of happiness. If you want to be happy, there are a certain number of things you must do... and a certain number of things you must not do. Happiness is like a gift, a talent, and it has to be cultivated. It is exactly the same as with an artistic talent: if you don't cultivate it, it will never amount to anything. Even if someone has a tremendous gift for music, painting or dance, for instance, it will never develop into anything worthwhile if he does not work at it seriously every day.

If you want happiness, don't just sit there and do nothing about it. You must go out and start looking for the elements that nourish it; and as these elements belong to the divine world, that is where you have to look for them. Once you find them, you will love everyone and everything and be loved in return; you will understand things better, and you will have the power to create and achieve your aspirations.

Chapter Two

# HAPPINESS IS NOT PLEASURE

The need to find happiness is very profoundly rooted in every human being. It is this fundamental need that drives them and guides their actions. And even though each individual envisages happiness differently depending on his own particular temperament, most people think of it as pleasure, for happiness is always accompanied by pleasure. So much so, in fact, that most people fail to distinguish one from the other. They imagine that whatever pleases, attracts or interests them will make them happy. But that is not so; if you analyse pleasure and see what it really is and how and where you find it, you will soon see that the question is far more complicated.

When you consider how much energy human beings expend on activities that give them pleasure, it is obvious that if happiness were synonymous with pleasure the whole world would be overflowing with happiness. But what we see is

just the opposite. The things that give human
beings pleasure are very often the things that bring
them unhappiness.

Pleasure is a brief and very agreeable sensation
which leads you to believe that if only you could
prolong it indefinitely you would be happy. This
is an illusion. Why? Because the activities that give
you an agreeable sensation quickly and effortlessly
almost never belong to a very high plane. They
concern principally your physical body; they have
little to say to your heart, and practically nothing
to your mind. But no human being can be happy
if he seeks to satisfy only his physical body, or even
his heart and mind, for such satisfactions are
necessarily incomplete and transitory. Happiness,
unlike pleasure, is not a fleeting sensation; it is
something that concerns the whole of one's being.

He who thinks he will find satisfaction in
pleasure is like an alcoholic. When he pours a glass
of wine or spirits down his throat he feels on top
of the world. He forgets all his cares and concludes
that drinking is a magnificent pastime. Yes, it may
seem magnificent if you consider only the first few
minutes or hours of euphoria. But what about the
effects that will make themselves felt a few years
hence? The gradual loss of his mental faculties, the
incapacity for a normal social or family life, a loss
of reputation, even a recourse to crime. Yes, in
many circumstances, people behave like confirmed

drunkards; something gives them pleasure for a moment, and they conclude that it will continue to do so forever. But unfortunately they will eventually begin to see all that they have lost and all the damage they have done, and then they will suffer.

The same thing applies when it comes to choosing a friend, a marriage partner or a business associate. People tend to be guided by their instinctive likes or dislikes, their first feelings of sympathy or antipathy. They think, 'Ah, I like the look of that fellow,' and without reasoning or examining the question any further, they go into partnership with him. Only later do they find out that they are in partnership with a crook. And, by the same token, they will often reject a good, just and honest man simply because they don't like the look of him. As long as people continue to be guided by their spontaneous likes and dislikes – which are no more than the impressions of a moment – rather than by wisdom which is so much more far-sighted, they will continue to act foolishly and hurt themselves.

Initiates and sages warn us about the reality of things. They say, 'Be careful about what you choose to do: once the first moment of satisfaction has faded, you will have to pay dearly for your shortsightedness.' So many things are pleasurable for a short time, but what about the long term? For a few minutes of pleasure snatched here and there, you will have to endure years of suffering. This is why you must be vigilant and always a little distrustful of things that seem very pleasant.

It is true that certain pleasures can nourish the soul and spirit, but these are not the pleasures that human beings are most inclined to choose. Besides, it is always dangerous to be guided by pleasure, for the things that give men pleasure are usually the things that feed their instincts, not their souls or spirits. You only have to see what those things are: eating, drinking, sleeping with anyone who is willing, gambling, eliminating their business rivals, revenging themselves and so forth; the possibilities are almost infinite. But where is all this leading them? Certainly not in the direction of happiness, for happiness is something vast, something infinite, whereas pleasure only reaches a very small part of man, the paltry, selfish part that belongs to his lower nature.

In seeking pleasure, man is thinking primarily of himself, for his pleasure is himself. He is not thinking about anyone else's pleasure, only his own. And because he often has to resort to dishonourable means in order to obtain and defend his pleasure, he diminishes and defiles himself and becomes unjust and cruel to others. If anything deprives him of his pleasure, even momentarily, he is immediately irritable, aggressive and vindictive.

So where is the happiness he professes to find in these things? Other people find him unbearable and make no bones about letting him know it.

To be sure, I am not saying that you have to deprive yourself of every satisfaction and every pleasure; that would be stupid. It is nature herself, after all, that impels human beings to seek pleasure; without it life would lose all meaning and become indescribably dreary and monotonous. It is pleasure that animates and lends colour to life, so there is no question of wanting to do away with it. The only thing is that it must not have first place in your considerations; you must not make it your goal. On the contrary, the natural inclination for pleasure must be used constructively.

We all have instincts and desires, that is normal, but it is no reason to give in to those instincts and do only what gives us pleasure. If heaven has given us a brain, it is so that it may steer us in the right direction. A human being is like a ship sailing on the ocean of life. Below-decks is a crew of ordinary seamen whose job it is to keep the boilers stoked so that the ship can keep moving, and at the helm is the captain, who has a compass which enables him to keep the ship on course. The stokers are our instincts and appetites; they are blind, but they provide the power to keep us moving. And the captain is our intelligence, the wisdom at the helm that steers our ship in the right direction and makes sure that it does not strike a rock and sink or collide with another ship. Unfortunately, many of the human 'ships' we see are sinking because their captains have allowed the crew to do whatever they pleased.

Bitter disillusionment awaits those whose judgement and behaviour are ruled by the pleasure principle, for they cannot foresee the future consequences of the choices they make today. Reason, not pleasure, should be your guide, for reason can tell you exactly where each step in any direction will take you, and it will warn you: 'Careful! That way lies danger. ' or 'Go ahead; you're on the right path.' If you talk to people about this, you will discover that, unfortunately, most of them are convinced that they can fulfil themselves only by doing what gives them pleasure. In fact, they are ready to flout every law and every 'taboo,' as they say, in the process. They want to be free. But what is this freedom they are asking for? The freedom to commit every imaginable folly and even to destroy themselves. For when someone frees himself – as he thinks – from light, wisdom and reason for the sake of a few moments of pleasure, the inevitable result is suffering. Suffering even on the physical plane. He will fall ill, for illness is simply the physical manifestation of a disorder that has been allowed to take hold on the psychic plane.

There is nothing wrong in wanting to overthrow the prejudices and restrictions of a rigid moral code in order to be fully oneself; on the contrary. But it is essential to realize that there are other moral laws on a higher plane than those of man. These are the eternal laws laid down by cosmic intelligence, and whether we like it or not, anyone who transgresses these laws will have to pay the penalty in grief, suffering and illness. As I have been telling you for a long time: it is easy to foresee that mankind is going to suffer from all kinds of new diseases because of the way human beings use their freedom. And some of those diseases will be incurable.

Of course, cosmic intelligence is not so cruel as to condemn anyone immediately for the least little fault. Someone who is too fond of food, drink, tobacco or sexual pleasure, for instance, may fall ill only after years and years of over-indulgence. But it is still a foregone conclusion that if his behaviour does not change very rapidly, he will not escape the scourge of illness. The physical organism of someone who oversteps the mark in whatever sphere is like the framework of a house that is being eaten away by woodworm: it is not destroyed from one day to the next but, after years and years, the whole house suddenly collapses. Many things in life are like that, and as people don't understand how the laws work, they base their reasoning on too short a period of time. They say, 'Look at this man, here. He's honest, sensible and kind, but that hasn't done him any good. Whereas that one, over there, is a confirmed scoundrel and succeeds in everything he does.' And they conclude that it is to their advantage to be a scoundrel. This is the philosophy that prevails in the world today: people can see no further than the end of their nose.

In reality, if you want to understand how the laws work, you have to be able to observe beings and events over a long period of time. A brief segment of time is not enough; it does not give you the elements you need to form a judgement. Look at how things work out in the history of a country, for example; it is only after centuries that you can see exactly how a country gradually fell into decadence. Those who lived through that decadence could not see what was happening. And the same holds true for human beings. We may not always be able to see the consequences of our actions, whether good or bad, in our present incarnation; we may have to wait for our next incarnation.

Yes, unfortunately – or fortunately perhaps – man's happiness does not lie in doing exactly what he pleases, as and when he pleases. As I have said: happiness is not pleasure. Be careful, therefore; don't let yourselves be deceived. A great many people who have always thought it normal to

respect certain rules of conduct first begin to defy
those rules because others scoff at them and tell
them that they should liberate themselves from
such ridiculous nonsense. Eventually, they are so
'liberated' that they come to a very bad end. And
this happens to so many people who believe
themselves to be highly intelligent. Their lives end
in disaster. And not only their own lives, but also
the lives of all the naïve and gullible people who
follow them. You all know the parable in the
Gospels about the blind man: if the blind leads the
blind, both will fall into a ditch. Yes, but this is a
very frequent phenomenon. So many scholars,
philosophers and thinkers proclaim all kinds of
theories that are completely absurd, and yet
everybody follows them. Whereas, in spite of the
fact that Initiates can explain the very foundations
on which life is built, people refuse to listen to
them; in fact, they flee from them. Why? The
reason is simple; it is because the things that
Initiates talk about are never particularly agreeable.
They talk about laws, reason, wisdom and self-
control. Even about sacrifice. Whereas others talk
about desire, pleasure and passion, and naturally
everybody finds this more to their liking. Yes, but
what an Initiate tells you is really and truly for your
good. Perhaps not for what you consider to be your
good, now, at the moment, but for your long-term,
ultimate, eternal good. The only trouble is, of

course, that you cannot see this. You are blind. And
this is real blindness: to see only the present
moment and the immediate gratification of a desire,
a need or an instinct, instead of seeing a more
distant future.

I realize, of course, that these explanations may
not be suitable for all; we have to allow people to
seek happiness in their own way. Everyone is sure
to find a few crumbs to stay the pangs of hunger.
Nature is so generous and open-handed. She has
left a few titbits in all kinds of places; even in
rubbish bins – figuratively speaking. Why should
those who are incapable of finding nourishment
elsewhere be forced to die of hunger by being
deprived of the only kinds of food for which they
have an appetite? Of course, they will perhaps
make themselves ill with the food they choose, but
what can anyone do about it, if that is the only kind
they want?

And what about those who sense that fulfilment
and happiness lie elsewhere, and who truly desire
to seek them out? They must be given the help they
need. They must be told, 'It is very difficult to
obtain happiness, true happiness, but it is not
impossible. It takes a great deal of work, a great
deal of will-power, and above all a great deal of
discernment. You have to understand that what
most human beings call 'happiness' amounts to no
more than a few moments of pleasure and

gratification; a mere semblance of happiness. If you want to embark on the long and painful path that leads to true happiness – and once you have obtained it, to give it to others – then you must look for it off the beaten path; in things other than pleasure.'

Chapter Three

# HAPPINESS IS FOUND IN WORK

Where is the greatest danger for an alcoholic? In alcohol? No; in his mind. Why? Because he perceives everything in terms of the momentary pleasure it gives him. While he is actually drinking he feels on top of the world and draws the magnificent conclusion that it will always be like this. But that is where he is mistaken, for although there is nothing more wonderful than pleasure in the short term, in the long term it spells ruin.

You will say, 'All right, we've all understood that it is not pleasure that will give us happiness. But what will?' And my answer to that is: 'Work!' And, there again, I know what you are going to say. You are going to complain that I want to deprive you of every joy or satisfaction; that you never do anything but work and that it is sheer drudgery; in other words, that work does not make you happy at all. Well, the only thing this proves is that you have not yet understood what work really is. If you had, you would know that it is in work that you will find happiness.

To replace pleasure by work is to replace an ordinary, selfish activity by one that is nobler and more generous, one that expands your consciousness and opens you to new possibilities. It is not a question of depriving yourself of all pleasure, but simply of not giving it priority, of not making it the goal of your existence, for it inevitably weakens and impoverishes those who do so. He who seeks pleasure before everything else is like someone who tries to keep warm in winter by throwing all his furniture and everything that is made of wood onto the fire. Doors, windows, chairs, beds, cupboards... everything is consumed by the flames. Before long he has nothing left. This is exactly what happens to those who are guided exclusively by the pleasure principle; the emotions and sensations that warm them today burn up all their reserves. Those who seek pleasure at all costs, therefore, must be warned in advance that the end result can only be great inner poverty and confusion and a dulling of their consciousness. They will never know the treasures of the soul and spirit, only the sensations and demands of their stomach, their belly, their sexual organs.

Instead of making pleasure the goal of your existence, therefore, you must make work your goal. In other words, you must replace pleasure with an ideal and make up your mind to do something sensible and noble with your life;

resolve to do some serious, useful work. And what is this work? It is the work of the sun. I have never discovered any activity superior to that of the sun, for the sun spends all its time radiating light, warmth and life. Human beings have never taken the sun's work seriously: they are only interested in worthless trifles.

One day, in spite of the clumsiness and imperfection of their first attempts, disciples who seriously decide to adopt the same profession as the sun will begin to radiate the same light, heat and life as the sun. Once they undertake this work, other activities begin to appeal to them less and less. All those mean little pleasures, all those trivial amusements pale before the glorious task of working as the sun works. Then they experience a pleasure, a joy and fulfilment that nothing can match.

Many people are resigned to the idea that happiness is nothing more than a few moments of effervescence, a brief flash in the pan, followed by grief and despair. Well, if happiness were no more than that, it would certainly not be worth seeking. What is the good of something so volatile? This reminds me... Do you know when I discovered that the French were the most intelligent people in the world? The day I first heard someone in Paris singing *Plaisirs d'amour*: 'The pleasures of love only last for a moment; the anguish of love lasts all your life.' I had never heard that in Bulgaria. It is because the French discovered this that I have such a high regard for them. The only thing is, I wonder why, having discovered this important truth, they continue to behave as though they had never discovered anything at all.

The fact is that once you have discovered love, true love, nothing and no one can ever take it away from you; it is yours for ever. You will say, 'Yes, but when you love someone, how can you replace love with work? It's not possible.' Indeed, it is. What is to stop you holding your beloved in your arms and concentrating together on light, beauty and eternal life, without going any further? To be sure, there are people for whom this would be impossible, because they are convinced that sensual pleasure must rule their lives. But if those of you who are here today begin to study and practise this new approach, you will see for yourselves that you are making progress, that you are beginning to develop other faculties, that you are beginning to enjoy subtler forms of pleasure.

Sensual pleasures are agreeable to begin with, of course, but little by little they destroy you. Work, on the other hand, is painful to begin with, but as time goes on you become tireless, rich and happy. It is in your own best interest, therefore, to make work your goal in life, that is to say, to make every moment of the day an occasion to advance and grow in self-mastery, harmony and light. And you will see that it is in this work that, one day, you will find the most exquisite pleasure.

But, here too, you must not be misled by immediate impressions, for those impressions are often deceptive. You must think carefully about the choices you make and look ahead to the long-term effects. You work and exert yourself every day, and at the moment you cannot see that your efforts are doing any good, so you get discouraged. Well, what you see may be true at the moment, but if you could see – as I can – the magnificent future that all your hard work is preparing, you would never want to stop.

Chapter Four

# A PHILOSOPHY OF EFFORT

Human beings have an inborn tendency to avoid effort of any kind. They will do everything possible to get others – other human beings, animals or machines – to do their work for them. And the more they do this, the weaker they become and the more their faculties waste away. If you want to become strong, resourceful and capable of facing up to every occasion you must get into the habit of exerting yourself. It is our efforts that keep us upright and alive. It is easy to acquire all kinds of possessions today without making the slightest effort, but what will be the result of this facility? We shall have everything we desire on the outside, but inwardly we shall be hollow, empty.

There is no denying that technical progress has made a great many things much easier. But, at the same time, the things that are the most vital to our survival – the soil, air and water – are more and more polluted, and the toxic elements we are continually forced to absorb are rapidly contaminating us. All this progress, therefore, is not really contributing much to the true development, the true happiness of humankind. On the contrary, it is contributing, above all, to undermining man's strength by making it unnecessary for him to exert himself. Yes, people have machines that work for them, do their calculations for them, remember things for them, move about for them, and in the meantime, they are quite simply degenerating. They have built all kinds of machines in order to move over the earth or in the air; their planes, helicopters and rockets carry them into space, but they are still inwardly earthbound, incapable of loosening their bonds and rising mentally to a higher plane.

There is absolutely no reason why you should not use all the technical means available to you – or even invent others if you are capable of doing so – but you must begin by doing the inner work that will enable you to use them in order to become richer, instead of letting them continue to make you weaker and poorer. However great your power, glory or wealth, you will never get any real satisfaction from it if it has never required an effort. It is on your own efforts that you must count; it is in your own efforts that you will find happiness and joy. For it is yourself and your own activity that provides the only solid foundation on which to build your life. As long as you fail to understand this you will never be in control of your own life. You will continually depend on external conditions; you will continually be at the mercy of shifting circumstances, and you will never obtain the things you most deeply desire. Everything will slip through your fingers. Get into the habit, therefore, of relying only on your own efforts and heaven and earth will be yours; nothing will ever disappoint you.

You will say, 'But we already make all kinds of efforts; we never do anything else. We have to make an effort day after day in order to earn a living.' Yes, that is true; but it is not enough. In any case, I am not talking about efforts of that kind. I am talking about the effort of heart, soul and spirit, the effort you must make to get back to your true self, to link yourself to the essential core of your own being: your higher self. This is the one most important effort you can make, and whatever else happens, you must persevere in it every day. Even if you fail to achieve the ideal you are striving for you must never waver in this endeavour, for the efforts you impose on yourself in order to develop and grow to your full potential are the only things that will remain with you beyond death. They are the key to your future.

This is why, when you encounter difficulties in your life, you must neither rebel against them nor try to dodge them. Instead, you must understand that cosmic intelligence has placed you in these particular circumstances in order to stimulate you to go much further and much higher. Don't ask for life to be smooth. A mountaineer could never reach the peak if the face of the mountain were perfectly smooth. He needs the handholds and footholds that the rough, jagged bits give him; he needs the crevices and rocky excrescences to fasten his rope to. It is thanks to them that he manages, little by little, to reach the top. In exactly the same way, this is why we need the difficulties, griefs and obstacles we meet in life.

You will probably feel like objecting that there is a contradiction here. I keep telling you that life must be harmonious and peaceful, and now I am saying that we need to encounter difficulties and opposition in order to advance. But there is one thing you have to understand, and that is that those who hope for a life of harmony and peace without having learned, first of all, to overcome obstacles are, on the contrary, laying the foundations of a life of disorder and contradictions. Why? Because true harmony and true peace are a reward, and they are bestowed only on those who have earned them by manifesting qualities of disinterestedness, kindness and patience. In such cases, even if they still have many trials, they are not troubled by them. They neither suffer nor cause others to suffer, because they have learned to transform, improve and make use of everything. Thanks to their patient, sustained efforts they establish a relationship of exchange with heaven, they are in communication with all its luminous inhabitants, and one day they find themselves swept up to the very summit. They no longer need to drag themselves painfully up the mountain side by means of life's asperities. They fly. Is this so difficult to understand?

Obviously, man is right to aim for happiness, fulfilment and peace, for these are the marks of true life; but he will never reach his goal as long as he is still too imperfect. Do I need to prove this to you? Is there anyone on earth who does not long for happiness? Human beings wish for nothing else; they spend their lives plotting and planning how to get the things that they mistakenly believe will make them happy... and yet they are never happy. So we have to conclude that there is still something wrong with the way they go about things, something that still needs to be understood and adjusted. Yes, as long as you have never made any effort to advance on the path of perfection, there is no point in expecting life to be smooth and pleasant. It won't be. You must accept all the difficulties that come along, therefore, knowing that it is the efforts you impose on yourselves that will lead to true happiness.

I know that it is hard for you to admit it, but this is the reality. If things happened according to your wishes, the result would often be catastrophic. Human beings are not sufficiently clear-sighted to see the long-term consequences of what they wish for. If the things they believed to be for their good all came to pass, they would end by living a life of idleness and pleasure. It is just as well that cosmic intelligence does not give human beings the kind of happiness they want: if it did they would lose everything, including all zest for life. Yes, because happiness is in the efforts we make. Stop asking for things to be sweet and sugary, for they will only make you ill. The day you develop a taste for bitterness, for quinine, you will be on the road to salvation. Don't cry for the things you like and cannot have, for they are often the things that would make you ill. If heaven deprives you of them it is so that you shall live a little longer.

This is the true philosophy, the philosophy that I have received and accepted. It is my philosophy and I would not abandon it for all the wealth in the world. Of course, that does not mean that if someone came and offered me wealth I would refuse it. I welcome anything that can be useful and made to serve others, but I am not looking for wealth.

So there you have the one thing that is essential: to make every effort possible in order to advance and come closer to attaining your ideal. Perhaps you will not gain much on the material external level in this way, but even kings and princes will not have the inner wealth you will have. Don't allow yourselves to be permanently subjugated by outward appearances. If you want true wealth, infinite wealth, you have to look for it inwardly. When you begin to make this effort, light will come, power will come, order and harmony will come.

Human beings are always fascinated by the external aspects of reality: even in their moments of silent reflection, their minds are occupied with external objects and events. Yes, even when they are immersed in reflection, instead of focusing on the reality that lies hidden deep in the centre of their being, they think about events in the outer dimension. And you are no exception. Analyse yourselves and you will find that you are incapable of entering into yourselves and remaining there for any length of time. Your attention is always being drawn to the outside world. You will complain that what I am asking you to do is too difficult. Perhaps, but it is good for you to hear this, for one day you will remember it and discover that, at last, you are truly capable of genuine inner life.

Build your existence on your own efforts; rely on nothing else. Accept and use whatever is good in the outside world, but don't pin your faith on it. You are destined, in the future, to travel throughout every region of space, to visit the stars and the suns, and the only things you will be able to take with you on the voyage will be the wealth that you have

managed to store up inwardly. You must learn what
to work at and what to rely on. As long as you rely
on your husband or children, on your house or your
money, sooner or later you are bound to be
disappointed. The only thing you can really count
on is the spirit, the spirit that is pure activity,
unrelenting effort. As for the rest, use it if you have
it and be grateful for what heaven has given you,
but don't rely on it.

I will go even further, and tell you that you must
not rely on your Master. As long as you see me as
existing outside yourself, as someone who is
sometimes with you and sometimes not, you cannot
rely on me. But if you keep me within you, if I am
always in your heart and soul, then, to be sure, you
can count on me, because my presence within you
will be as faithful and true as you yourself. When
you suffer distress and pain, I shall always be there
to help you. You will sense that I am with you
wherever you go; that I never leave you alone; that
something of my own knowledge, love and
patience has been infused into your being. You will
say, 'But in that case is there any point in coming
here to these meetings?' Yes, it is good to come;
these meetings can be useful and you should take
advantage of them, but don't rely exclusively on
them. If you do that you are bound to be unhappy
and disillusioned in the long run.

Chapter Five

# LIGHT MAKES FOR HAPPINESS

Most people know, deep down within themselves, that money cannot give them true happiness. The French have the saying, 'Money doesn't make for happiness.' At the same time, however, people realize that money enables them to satisfy many of their desires. And, as they always have a great many desires, they obviously need a great deal of money. But there is just one question to be considered – and a very important question it is – and that is whether the desires that can be satisfied with money are, for the most part, highly disinterested and elevated?

Be careful, therefore. Always ask yourselves why you want money and what you intend to use it for. Yes, this is the point that needs to be watched, for money is the most powerful means of satisfying your lower nature. Your divine nature has no use for money; it needs light, love, infinity and eternity, and these things cannot be bought with money.

Money can only give you the things you need on the material plane: food, clothes, jewellery, houses, cars, etc. Nothing else. As often as not it cannot even be used to improve your health. When you are deeply disturbed and distressed and have lost all interest in life even the most expensive medicine cannot cure you. Or, if it does give you a little relief, the chaotic, disordered life you lead is enough to neutralize all its good effects and make you ill all over again. For the fault lies in the way you live, and you can only cure it with something that cannot be bought.

Of course, money is necessary; you won't hear me telling you that you can do without it, for you would simply become social parasites. And the problem cannot be solved, as some people think, by doing away with money which, they say, is the cause of all the ills of society. Money is simply a means of exchange, and if we did away with it we would have to put some other form of currency in its place, for society is based on barter, on the exchange of goods and services, and we would find ourselves faced with exactly the same problem. If money is used destructively it is not the money that is to blame, but the person who uses it in order to satisfy his own ignoble appetites. If someone has evil intentions in mind, he can use money as a tool to help him carry them out. If he had other, divine ideas in mind, that same money could become a blessing in his hands.

Money has extraordinary power over our lower nature. It excites it and eggs it on: 'Go on, go on!

You have what you need to ruin this one, to supplant that one. The woman you love is already married? Don't let that deter you: if you want her you can have her. She won't be able to resist the car or the diamonds you give her.' Yes, money is an evil counsellor and the personality is all too ready to listen to it; you can see it happening every day. If you really want to know what someone is like, give him a lot of money and observe his reactions. If he does not immediately throw himself into a round of pleasure; if he does not immediately show himself to be arrogant, vain, exacting and despotic, it proves that he is someone really worthwhile. He is someone who can be counted on, for he has overcome the temptations that money offers.

To clear up this question once and for all, you must understand that the danger lies in allowing money to occupy your head. By this, I mean that you must not keep thinking about money, for the idea of it and the desire for it can grow and swell to such proportions that the sky itself is blocked out. Money becomes a screen that prevents the light of heaven from entering and dwelling within you. I do not deny that it is a good thing to have money, but only on condition that you keep it in your pocket, in a drawer or in a safe, so that you can get at it when you need it. On condition, in other words, that you keep it anywhere but in your head;

otherwise it will become your master and you will
be its slave. If you are the master, if you make your
money obey you, you can do a lot of good with
it; but if you are its slave, it will force you to
oppress and destroy your fellow men. And then,
even though the masses may applaud your success
as a banker or a brilliant businessman with factories
and offices throughout the world, and ignore the
fact that you have trampled on all the laws of
kindness, generosity and disinterestedness in your
climb to the top, divine justice will eventually catch
up with you and you will have to account for your
actions. You will have to pay for your
transgressions with all kinds of physical and
psychological suffering.

It is up to each one of you to reflect on the
attitude you should have with regard to money, and
above all to avoid making it an ideal, a goal in life.
Avoid letting it dwell in your head so that it
becomes a screen that prevents the sun, the spirit,
from filling you with light. Your head must be at
the disposal only of heaven, the angels and
archangels; it must be free and ready to receive the
messages and guidance they send you. If you have
a screen in your head, these messages will be
deflected and you will never know which way to
turn; there will be no one to guide you. And when
man is not guided, he falls head first over a cliff or
into an ambush.

If you want happiness, it is not money you need but light. People sometimes come and consult me about what profession to choose. They often hesitate between a very lucrative profession and one that is less highly paid but that would leave them freer to do other things as well. And what do you suppose I tell them? The fact that I am their instructor does not mean that I have to tell them what to do; my role is simply to explain what the consequences of their choice will be. Then it is up to them to reflect and analyse themselves carefully and make up their own minds. So what I tell them is this: 'There is nothing wrong in wanting to make a lot of money, but it all depends on your goal, your ideal, on what you want to achieve in life. If your ambition is to achieve what most people think of as "success," that is to say, to become powerful and influential, then by all means make a lot of money. But if your ideal is to make progress in your inner life, to grow spiritually, your material needs will not be so great and you will be perfectly happy with less money. The choice is yours.'

In any case, someone who has a great deal of money never has a very peaceful life; he lives in a constant turmoil of activity and stress and has to be permanently on guard against the many ambitious, deceitful, greedy people who would like to relieve him of some of his wealth. And how can he ever be sure that his precautions will protect him against every eventuality? All these preoccupations weigh him down and materialize him and cut him off from the spiritual dimension. What a terrible waste of time and energy that could be more usefully employed in furthering his own evolution and in using every opportunity that arises to help others with his own spiritual acquisitions. Whatever your work may be, therefore, you would do better not to overburden yourselves but be content to have no more than the necessities of life. To ask for more only makes life more complicated.

Perhaps you are wondering whether it is a danger for a person's evolution to inherit a great fortune. Well, in the first place, such cases are not as numerous as all that, and in any case, it all depends on the person, on whether he uses his fortune to satisfy the impulses of his lower nature, his personal ambition or his slothful inclinations, or whether he is disinterested, in control of his impulses and capable of using his fortune for the good of those around him.

In the final analysis, however, you must always remember that money is useful only on the material plane. You cannot do anything useful with it on the psychic or spiritual plane; on this plane the currency you need is light, the light that is fluid gold. If you love light, it means that you already possess gold on the spiritual plane. And the more you possess of that gold, the more precious things

you can 'buy' with it in the 'shops' of heaven –
things that cannot be bought anywhere else, such
as wisdom, love, joy, infinity and eternity. This is
why sages and Initiates try to amass as much gold
as possible on the spiritual plane so as to be rich
in qualities and virtues that they can then distribute
to others. Even if their pockets are empty, thanks
to their fortune in light, they continually receive
precious gifts from heaven and distribute them to
those around them.

The question is quite clear, therefore: it is
preferable to be content with little on the material
plane and to be insatiable on the spiritual plane.
On that level, you must never be satisfied with what
you are or what you have; you must always strive
to become richer and richer, to be, more and more,
a power for good. And it is just too bad if this is
not in keeping with the moral or religious code of
the majority. According to that common or garden
'morality' it is enough to be a good husband and
father. To earn enough to feed and clothe one's wife
and children, to take them out for a drive on
Sundays and bring them all safely home in the
evening – this, we are told, should be our moral
ideal. Of course, such a 'morality' is not actually
bad; in fact, many people are not capable of doing
even that. But it is hopelessly inadequate for those
who want to live by the rules of true morality, true
religion.

True morality and true religion are contained in Jesus' precept: 'You shall be perfect, as your Father in heaven is perfect,' and how can you possibly be perfect if the moral code you live by is too pedestrian? The gulf between man and God is so great that one wonders why Jesus gave us such an ideal. It is beyond anything we could imagine: to be as perfect as God himself. Well, Jesus knew what he was saying. Yes, because, although we must be content to have very little in the way of material possessions – and be grateful for the little we have – on the spiritual plane we must never be content; we must always be insatiably ambitious, always striving for the highest and most unattainable ideal: divine perfection. We should want and ask for unlimited heavenly possessions. Yes, ask for one hundred per cent – so as to get at least one per cent. And the one thing you must ask for, above all others, is light. Ask that all your thoughts, all your feelings, everything you do and even your physical body be permeated, infused with light. Light... this one word sums up and condenses every imaginable good, all that is purest, most powerful, most beautiful and most sublime – God himself.

One day when I was very young and had recently made the acquaintance of the Master Peter Deunov, I asked him, 'Master, what is the best way to be in close touch with God while one is meditating?' His answer was this: 'The best way is to work with light, for light is an expression of divine splendour. You have to concentrate on light and work with it. Steep yourself in it, rejoice in it. It is through light that we can be in contact with God.' So, this is what I say to you, too. There is no work to equal the work with light. Light is a vibrant, pulsating ocean of life; you can dive into it, you can swim and purify yourself in it, you can drink it and be nourished by it. It is in the midst of light that you will find total fulfilment.

Light is also a symbol of all the different colours and you can work with light by concentrating on each colour separately or in combination with others. Once you have learned to create colours mentally, you can send beams of coloured light through your own being and out to those you love and to the whole world. This work with light is a work with virtues, forces and heavenly entities, for light is the visible manifestation of an abundant, invisible life. When you work with colours you enter into communication with that life.

At about the same time, the Master Peter Deunov said something else that I have never forgotten either. In those days, before the Brotherhood began to meet at Izgrev, on the outskirts of the town, he gave his lectures in a meeting room on Oborichte Street in Sofia. One day, a man had come to talk to him before the lecture, and was asking him all kinds of questions. I was there, listening. The Master was always very simple and natural, very dignified and serious. He would answer people's questions kindly but very briefly. At one point the man asked him, 'How can you tell whether someone is highly evolved or not?' and the Master replied, 'By the intensity of the light emanating from him.' I was very young and this criterion was completely unknown to me at the time. But I was so struck by it that once I heard it I based the greater part of my life on it. Throughout my life, I too have found that one can judge people by the light emanating from them.

Of course, this light is not physically visible, but it can be sensed in a person's eyes, in his facial expression, in the harmony of his gestures. It has nothing to do with his intellectual faculties or his education; it is a manifestation of divine life. And this is the light that we must hunger after and seek persistently, unremittingly, insatiably.

Chapter Six

# THE MEANING OF LIFE

Every human being, whoever he may be – and whether he knows it or not – seeks to give meaning to his life. He needs to have a reason for existing, and he looks for this reason among all his different experiences and the different aspects of his family, social and professional life. But in reality, neither personal success nor material possessions can ever reveal to him the meaning of life, precisely because a meaning is not material; it can only be found on a much higher level, on the subtlest planes of existence. Here on the physical plane we can only find forms. Forms can, of course, be filled with content, the content that comes from the feelings and sensations born of a great love for an object, a being or an activity. But feelings are transitory, and sooner or later, they disappear and leave us to suffer from the void that remains within. So we need to go and look for something that is beyond content. We need to look for meaning. Once you have found meaning you have found fulfilment.

An example will, perhaps, help you to understand what I am trying to explain. Yesterday

you ate a very good meal, but that meal was for
yesterday and today you need to eat again. The
memory of yesterday's meal cannot satisfy today's
hunger. But if, when reading a book, looking at a
painting or listening to some music, for example,
you suddenly sense that you have discovered a truth
that transforms your vision of reality, that revelation
will still be with you tomorrow and the day after.
This is because that book, painting or piece of
music is a medium through which your spirit rises
to a higher plane and perceives a meaning. And
that meaning is an eternal element that enters into
your being and never leaves you again.

Once you have found the meaning of things it
is yours for ever, but in order to find it you have to
rise to a great height and eat, think, love and act
on the higher planes. It is no good looking for
meaning on too low a level, for you will never find
it; material things cannot reveal it to you. Whereas,
if you possess a truth that somebody has revealed
to you or that you have discovered for yourself,
you can live with it and work with it every day and
you will get results.

Obviously, an occasional moment of inspiration
or illumination is not enough to give meaning to
your life. You also have to learn to make such
moments last so that they become a permanent state
of consciousness capable of purifying and restoring
order and harmony to your whole being.

Unfortunately, you are often so heedless and superficial that you switch, in a matter of moments, from the divine world to the most prosaic and foolish concerns, and it is as though you wiped out all that had gone before. You simply don't know how much you lose in this way, for that state of illumination was capable of influencing the whole of your being, of sweetening and harmonizing every inner movement. If you had been able to sustain it, it would have had the power to prevent certain negative states from slipping in and taking possession of you. But there you are... You are always looking for variety, for a change, so you go from meditation or prayer straight back to thinking about all kinds of rubbish, to planning a dishonest business transaction, to thoughts of revenge or of pleasure.

You will say, 'But you are asking the impossible. No one can sustain a divine state of consciousness in the life we live today.' Yes, to all appearances, you are right. I know what you mean because I live in the same world as you, and I know what it is like. But I also know that, whatever the circumstances and in spite of every kind of fatigue, discouragement, sorrow or misfortune, a disciple of the light will never let go. On the contrary, he clings to all the great and beautiful experiences he has had, to those special moments of grace that have shown him the true meaning of life.

So although it is impossible to go through life without sometimes suffering and weeping, you must always safeguard this meaning within yourselves. And not only safeguard it, but make use of all the difficulties of your everyday lives to reinforce and amplify it. This is how truly spiritual people work. Whatever happens, they never allow their divine inner work to be interrupted. For them, even the most terrible tribulations are an occasion to mobilize and harness these hostile forces to their work. Most human beings, on the other hand, behave so irresponsibly that, although nothing very terrible happens to them, they demolish any good they may have achieved. They build up something and immediately tear it down, build up and tear down... Is it any wonder that they never get any results? If you want results, you must nurture the spiritual work you undertake; that is to say, you must make everything contribute to that work, all good and all evil, all your joys and sorrows, all your hopes and all your despair. Everything must serve your work. This is the only way to build, for every day adds new elements to the edifice.

Neither your family life nor your profession, neither art nor travel nor any other activity can give you the meaning of life. They can be the means that help you to come closer to it, but they do not contain it in themselves. And to be convinced of this, you only have to realize that none of these things – the family, the profession, art or travel – has ever prevented a man or woman from committing suicide.

You will find the meaning of life when you make up your minds to work for the coming of the kingdom of God and his righteousness on earth. For, when you do this, you will always know that, whatever happens, you are a worker in the Lord's vineyard; you will always feel fulfilled, happy and full of courage simply because you are participating in such tremendous work. You will never be alone; never abandoned. Everybody can find the meaning of life, today, at once. Instead of working only for themselves, their own needs or their own satisfaction, everyone can say, 'Today and henceforth I'm going to work for the kingdom of God and his righteousness.' Even if they remain completely unknown on earth, their names will be inscribed in the book of life, and the blessings of heaven will fill them to overflowing. Nothing is more glorious than to commit oneself to this work. Yes, for you must always go further and higher, always aspire to something greater, something nobler and more far-reaching. This is what really gives meaning to life.

When you have experienced a moment of divine beauty, whether during meditation or prayer or when listening to music, reading or looking at some beautiful scenery, always try to appreciate it and thank heaven for it. Tell yourselves, 'This was a truly exceptional moment of grace. I must nurture it tomorrow and every day, for it was a moment of heaven itself. And this moment will transform my whole being.'

To find the meaning of life is to find an element that can only come from the divine world. But the divine world only gives it to those who, for years on end, make a sincere effort to find it. The meaning of life is not something that can be conjured up emotionally or mentally by man himself. It is not man who decides what the meaning of life will be for him.

The discovery of the meaning of life is a reward, a reward for a patient, persistent work of inner transformation. When a human being attains a certain level of consciousness he receives an electron, a gift from heaven, which, like a drop of light, impregnates every fibre of his being. From that moment his life acquires a new dimension and a new intensity; he sees events with a new clarity of vision as though he had received an understanding of the reason for all things. He has no more fear, even of death, because that atom, that electron he has received, has opened his eyes to the immensity of an eternal world in which danger and darkness no longer exist; he senses that he dwells already in the limitless world of light.

Once you have found the meaning of everything else pales in comparison, and the cares and sorrows of your everyday lives become far less important. Those who spend their time moaning and groaning because they never have enough money, because their hopes of success have been disappointed, because others have abandoned or betrayed them, are simply demonstrating that they have never discovered the true meaning of life. If, to them, life's meaning lies in money, success, the possession of a man or woman, then, of course, there will be no lack of occasions for disappointment and unhappiness.

To find the meaning of life is to attain a state of consciousness so elevated that it embraces the whole universe, and all the minor, petty details of life lose their consistency and fade to nothing. Even if he is despised and persecuted, a man who has found the meaning of life feels comforted within himself; it is he who looks at others with pity, thinking to himself, 'Poor creatures, they don't know that, whatever they say or do to me, I am living in immensity and eternity, I am participating in the life of the cosmos.'

Perhaps you find that what I have been saying is very difficult to understand. Actually, there is really only one thing you have to remember, and it is this: you will only find the meaning of life if you put yourself at the service of a sublime ideal.

For, behind that ideal, billions of luminous creatures are at work, and when they see that you want to collaborate in their work and build a new world with them, they will shower you with gifts and you will feel that something inside you is bursting and overflowing. Even if you ask for nothing and expect no reward, you will sense that you are being given everything.

Chapter Seven

# PEACE AND HAPPINESS

How often we hear people saying, 'How I wish they'd leave me in peace.' They imagine that if they were 'left in peace,' their problems would be solved and they could be happy. But what kind of peace are they talking about? Is it as easy as all that to be happy and in peace? No; people have no clear idea of what peace is. Any more than they have a clear idea of what happiness is.

When a human being is subject to his lower nature, to all his instincts, lusts and ambitions, he cannot live in peace. As long as any shreds of hatred, jealousy or avarice remain in his heart, mind or will, his life will be an endless series of conflicts and problems. Even though he may know some brief moments of respite when he thinks he has got what he wanted, other problems will soon arise and that will be the end of 'his' peace.

Neither is peace a matter of a few hours or days of quietness and tranquillity enjoyed when circumstances are particularly agreeable or when you are alone in the mountains. Peace, true peace such as Initiates understand it, is a higher state of consciousness that requires a knowledge of the

structure of man and of the universe. Yes, all the
Initiates will tell you that you will never really know
peace until all the elements of your different bodies
(physical, astral, mental, causal, buddhic and atmic)
have been purified and are in harmony with each
other, until the whole of your being vibrates in
unison with the loftiest spheres of the universe.

Peace, therefore, is a state of consciousness that
can be reached only after long years of sustained
effort to achieve self-mastery and inner
harmonization. Before reaching this final goal you
will certainly enjoy moments of quiet and
tranquillity, but you will never know true peace
until you have completed your work, for every day
– and several times a day – so many incidents occur
to trouble you. Once you have attained true peace,
those things will not matter any more. Even if you
do have all kinds of difficulties and misfortunes to
contend with, you will be unshaken. You may
sometimes be worried or unhappy perhaps, but
only on the surface. Deep down inside you, your
peace remains; you will feel that it is always there,
within you, as still and deep as the ocean bed that
remains untroubled by the storms that rage on the
surface. There is something immense, something
immeasurably vast and unalterable about peace,
for it is an acquisition of the soul and the spirit.

True peace belongs, therefore, to a very high
plane. It is an attunement, a synthesis, a harmoni-

zation of all the elements of our being. And the same is true of happiness. Those things that human beings mistake for happiness are often no more than small, fleeting satisfactions. You say that you are happy because you have had a wonderful vacation and are feeling rested and full of energy again, or because the man or woman you love has shown that your feelings are reciprocated, or because your intelligence and competence have earned you the congratulations of your colleagues, and so on. Of course, I don't deny that it is important to feel healthy and energetic, to know that you are loved or that your qualifications are appreciated, but these things are not enough to make you truly happy. True happiness belongs to a sphere beyond that of the physical body, the heart or the intellect. People are deluding themselves when they think that they would be happy if only they had a house or a wife; if only they had fame or great knowledge or beauty. No, thousands of years of history have shown us that these things do not bring happiness – or, if they do, only for a very short time. People acquire this and possess that and yet they are continually dissatisfied; inwardly they know only emptiness, a gaping void that threatens to swallow up everything.

If happiness is so difficult to obtain and hold on to, it is because it has to be sought on a very high plane, in a region in which materials are unchangeable. And this demands great qualities – particularly great purity – in those who seek it, for only that which is pure can endure without change or deterioration. This lofty region exists in space, but it also exists within us, and those who have already discovered it strive to think and love, to act and work in such a way as to dwell permanently in the shelter of its untroubled depths. Whatever the vicissitudes of life, however distressing their circumstances, they are happy because they have found something stable, immutable and eternal.

True happiness, like true peace, is a state characterized by stability. You will say, 'That's all very well, but life is an endless series of changes – success and failure, abundance and privation, peace and war, health and sickness – and man is necessarily subject to these changes.' No, you are wrong. War can break out, you can fall ill, you can suddenly lose all your money or be abandoned by your husband or wife, your children and your friends, without ceasing to be happy. Why? Because your consciousness is not content to stagnate on the level of events. Whatever difficulty or trial comes along, as you are capable of rising to a higher plane and know how to look at these things, you find an explanation, a truth that pacifies and consoles you. You can be stripped of all your possessions and persecuted without mercy, but since you know that all these things are temporary, that you yourself are immortal and that nothing can really reach you, trials that would overwhelm others leave you with a smile on your face.

Happiness, therefore, is already within you. If you are not conscious of it, it is because you live on the surface, on the outer edge of your own being, where all is illusion and flux. No sooner do you succeed in grasping a few shreds of joy, than they are torn from you and replaced by terrible sufferings, as though you had to be punished for stealing a little bit of happiness.

This is why you must make the effort to enter into yourselves and begin to look for all that is eternal and immutable, for the spirit, for God himself within you. If you do this you will find happiness. And once you have found it, cling to it so that no one will ever be able to make you unhappy again. Whatever your circumstances, whether you are rich or penniless, covered in glory or spat upon and covered with filth, much loved or much hated, you will soar above all vicissitudes; you will live in eternity.

Yes, I know: I don't expect this language to be understood by everybody. An ignorant little whippersnapper vows to make his sweetheart happy. But what does he know about happiness? He's not happy himself and yet he thinks he can make her happy. Or else it is the girl who promises, 'Darling, I'll always make you happy.' But how

can they make each other happy with all their
imperfections, all their irritability, anger and
jealousy? Yes, they imagine that they'll have a lot
of little ones and live happily ever after… a fairy-
tale life. No, no. That kind of happiness doesn't
inspire me with much confidence. To be sure, they
will have a few moments of joy together; but they
are like prisoners. Even prisoners are given a few
minutes of recreation every day in which to relax
and get a breath of fresh air before being sent back
to their cells. Or they are like people with
toothache; the pain eases for a few minutes and
then it begins all over again.

You cannot be happy unless you find something
stable and unchangeable to cling to so that nothing
can ever shake you or upset your balance again.
You have to reach what is known in physics as a
state of stable equilibrium. Look at a pendulum;
you can make it swing to left or right but it always
reverts to a state of equilibrium, because it is
suspended from something immovable. And man
needs to find and cling to this immovable point
of suspension within himself. When he finds this,
he will be in a position to echo the words of the
ancient Egyptian Initiate: 'I am stable, son of he
who is stable, conceived and engendered in the
realm of stability.'

It is pointless to speak of happiness as long as
you are still hesitant, unstable and changeable.

Happiness belongs to the spheres of infinity and eternity, which are the spheres of the soul and spirit. Yes... infinity and eternity. The soul and spirit need to penetrate into the depths of these two uncharted regions, for they are the only regions in which they can find the food and clothing they need, the only regions in which they can be fulfilled and totally free. You are now beginning to understand that your quest for happiness demands a real apprenticeship in which you learn to raise your understanding and love to the regions of the soul and spirit; only in this way will you be able to draw freely on that limitless ocean of peace and bliss. For peace, like happiness, is the result of a communion, of a perfect relationship of exchange with all the principles, entities and existences in the world of the soul and the spirit.

On the highest level, peace and happiness are one; they cannot exist apart from each other. You will never meet someone really happy who is not in peace. Peace and happiness are different expressions of the same reality. When you are in peace you are in harmony with the whole of creation and when you live in this harmony you cannot be unhappy. The energies and forces of the universe permeate your being; nothing is lacking to you.

You will never understand what happiness is if you are content to follow the majority and see it as no more than an agreeable sensation. True happiness is, certainly, a very agreeable sensation, but it is also light and power. Observe what happens when you are really happy, if only for a moment or two: you have a sense of peace, you begin to understand the events of your life, everything becomes clear and simple, and you succeed in all that you undertake. But as soon as that happiness slips away from you, you lose your sense of peace, you are the prey of sadness or discouragement, nothing is clear to you any longer and all your undertakings turn out disastrously.

Happiness is nothing but a state of consciousness, a way of understanding, feeling and behaving, an attitude to life. And this is why only those who know how to find it through spiritual work can grasp and hold on to it. Happiness, like peace, is a synthesis; if you understand and feel things correctly, you are in a position to act correctly and to be happy. But you can reach this goal only if you accept initiatic science, for only initiatic science teaches us how to train our intellect, heart and will, that is to say, how to master our lower nature, our personality, so that our higher nature, our individuality, may have every chance to grow and flower.

If you want to find happiness, it is not enough to conquer your lower nature. This conquest is necessary, to be sure, but it is insufficient. You must also fuse into one with your higher nature. Happiness will not be given to you just because you manage, every now and then, to overcome your selfishness, sensuality, jealousy and anger. Such minor victories are necessary steps on the road to happiness, but they cannot take you all the way, for happiness dwells in a region that is totally beyond the reach of anything negative. Besides, even if you do manage to conquer your personality one day, be on your guard, for it is perfectly capable of tripping you up badly the very next day.

The victory over one's personality can never be anything but precarious. It is like the victory of one country over another; you can never be sure that it will last. For while the conqueror is resting on his laurels, the conquered are busy preparing to take their revenge. And this is what happens with our lower nature, our personality; even if, in certain circumstances, you manage to repress some of its manifestations, your victory can never be final. Sooner or later it will rear up and unseat you and you will find yourselves flat on your back.

So what do you have to do? You have to implore your divine nature, the Christ-principle, to dwell permanently within you. In this way, instead of being a conqueror who can never be quite sure of his victory, you will always be able to count on the support of a powerful, omniscient ally. And even if you are sometimes a little tired or sleepy, this ally will continue to hold your lower nature in check. It so often happens that someone seems to have overcome certain weaknesses or vices and then, not long after, they regress and those same vices get an even stronger hold on them. The only solution, therefore, is to lay the groundwork of a final victory by gaining partial victories over your lower nature in as many areas as possible, and at the same time, to implore heaven, your higher nature, to come to you and manifest itself within you.

Once your higher nature is well and truly established within you, you will know a happiness that no words can describe. You will be happy without even knowing why. The most astonishing thing about this happiness is that it has no cause. You simply find that it is marvellous to be able to live and breathe, to eat and speak. No particular event seems to explain this happiness: no gifts, no rich inheritance, no special encounter. You just feel happy. Something has come into your life from above that does not even depend on you; it is like a stream pouring down from heaven, and you are astonished to discover that this marvellous state of consciousness is always there, within you. You are filled with joy without even knowing why. This is true happiness.

True happiness is like the air we breathe. Do you ever have to worry about going to look for air?

No, it comes to you of itself. It is just there; you are immersed in it and you breathe without even thinking about it. We often have to go and look for all the other things we need such as water, food or money, but we never need to look for air. Or for light. You breathe without ceasing and there is no greater joy than to breathe. And if you don't believe me, try holding your breath for a few minutes and you will see. Yes, happiness can be compared to the air we breathe.

To breathe in and breathe out... in and out... in and out. Happiness is the respiration of the soul. No one has ever paused to study respiration from this point of view. Everything else has to be looked for or bought, piece by piece, even joy or pleasure; but there is no need to go and look for air. We all breathe all the time, even when we are asleep. It is as though respiration had been given to man in order to show him that the tangible things of life such as money and possessions cannot compare with the subtle, intangible, invisible things, with the etheric world in which we are immersed. All those who are conscious of the fact that they are immersed in this etheric, spiritual world, breathe continually and are happy because of that respiration.

Chapter Eight

# IF YOU WANT TO BE HAPPY, BE ALIVE

If you want to be happy, you have to be alive. 'But we *are* alive.' you will say. Yes, you are alive, but animals are alive also, and always supposing that they are happy in their own way, do you think that you would be content with the happiness of an animal? That is not the life of man, his true life. So what is?

In our times, people attach much too much importance to intellectual activities and technical achievements. A formal education, the accumulation of knowledge and the advantages of technical progress are constantly being held up as an ideal. But life is not a question of storing up information and using more and more machines – or machines that are more and more sophisticated. In following this path, man is disrupting the natural order of things, and nature reacts in self-defence.

And what is the need that young people express so insistently today? Their desire to 'live.' Yes, but as their elders propose an ideal of life that has no appeal for them, and as they have no one to teach them what true life is, they look for it in all kinds of dangerous ways; in violent sensations, passion, pleasure, alcohol, drugs, and so on. So on the one hand there is too much intellect, and on the other, too much passion; in either case there is a lack of balance. You have to realize that man is designed to live concurrently on different planes, on the physical, astral and mental planes, but also on the causal, buddhic and atmic planes[1]. As long as he confines his activity to the three lower planes – physical, astral and mental – he will never know what true life is.

It is important to eat and drink, sleep, work and have sexual relations, to experience certain feelings, acquire a certain amount of knowledge and exchange ideas with others. Yes, these things are important, but they are incapable of satisfying all our needs. To confine yourselves to such things is to live in bottom gear; there is no intensity in such a life. You will say, 'How can you say that? People live very intense lives today. Look at them. They are always rushing about in all directions; always arguing, changing their husbands or wives, mistresses or lovers.' Yes, but you are letting yourselves be misled. The intensity of life has

---

[1] See Izvor Collection, No. 222, Man's Psychic Life; Elements and Structures, chap. 3.

nothing to do with hurry and bustle or with the number of your amorous adventures or your intellectual activities.

To live life with intensity requires, first of all, some understanding of the true structure of man. You have to know his different bodies and the subtle centres that enable him to communicate with the different regions of space and with the inhabitants of those regions. I have already talked to you about this and given you some indication as to the methods you can use, the exercises you can practise and the attitudes you should adopt in order to awaken your subtle organs[2]. Only those who are familiar with these things can claim to live the true life, the intense life. And in this intense life they are happy, because they sense that they are a living source, a fountain, an orchard of trees laden with fruit, a garden full of flowers… They are a benediction for all who come near them.

This is why I say to you that, if you are looking for happiness, the only secret to finding it is to live an intense spiritual life. It is useless to look for help from talismans or other magical objects, precious stones, metals, perfumes, etc., for the only true magic is life itself. If you want to be happy, work to make your life purer, richer and more fruitful.

---

2 See Izvor Collection, No. 219, Man's Subtle Bodies and Centres.

Once you work in this way on your physical body, your astral body (your feelings) and your mental body (your thoughts), you will immediately begin to see results. Your health will improve; you will feel the constant presence of love within you and all round you; each day the meaning of life will become clearer to you.

How do you set about this work? The whole of our teaching addresses this one question. For years I have been giving you methods – so many, in fact, that you could never put them all into practice. But choose at least a few of them and work with them seriously. Otherwise, if you do nothing, the years will go by and life will be obliged to take you in hand and teach you its own hard lessons. And this will involve much suffering. Believe me, you cannot be happy if you are content to live an ordinary, prosaic life.

And now, if you would like me to give you a method that you can start applying at once, here it is: get into the habit of saying, 'Thank you!' Yes, give thanks every moment of the day; give thanks whatever the circumstances. Be grateful always, even in the midst of difficulties, sorrow and suffering. In this way, all the poisons seeping into you from those negative influences will be neutralised and all your wounds will be healed, for gratitude is such a powerful remedy that nothing can resist it. Give thanks, therefore, until you reach the point where you sense that everything that happens to you is for your good. Starting now, say, 'Thank you, thank you, Lord!' Give thanks for all the things you have, but also for all the things you haven't got, for the things that give you pleasure and the things that give you pain. In this way you will be keeping alive the flame of life within you.

I can see that you are thinking to yourselves, 'Is that all?' Yes, that's all, but put this method into practice and you will see the results.

A genuine initiatic teaching teaches you to value life, your life, above all else. This may not strike you as something that is very important, because you don't realize that, in fact, you continually sacrifice your life to all kinds of things that are not nearly so precious. Your attention is always drawn to extraneous objects and events, to the tumult that goes on outside yourself, and in the meantime, you let your own life become poorer and poorer. And that is a most unprofitable way of behaving.

Have you ever thought about how much time you actually spend with the outside world? Only a few minutes or a few hours of the day. Whereas you are with yourself every minute of every day and every night. Isn't this enough to make you see that it is your inner life that is important? Abundance, wealth and order must be internal. The external world is teeming with a wealth of objects,

products, machines, buildings and weapons of
every sort and kind, while in the inner life of human
beings all is poverty, chaos, weakness and
emptiness. It is time they thought about achieving
inwardly all the things they devote so much time
to achieving outwardly. It is within ourselves that
we must have wealth, strength and beauty, for
nothing can take our inner possessions from us.
Not even old age.

Yes, I say this because most people think that,
once they begin to get old, they will necessarily
lose the use of their faculties and sink into senility.
They are so convinced of it, in fact, that it ends
by becoming true. Actually, the disciples of initiatic
science find that old age is the best period of their
lives, for years of research and inner experiences
have brought them lucidity, peace, serenity and
kindness. Others come to them to learn; even
children are drawn to them and love them. If the
general opinion is diametrically opposed to this, it
is because old age is indeed a sad time for many
people because of the way they have lived; they
have squandered their energies in all kinds of
mundane, futile, stupid activities, so that by the
time they are old they have nothing left. What can
they hope for in their old age if they are already
empty of all strength and health?

To be sure, however sensibly and intelligently
you live, old age will catch up with you in the end.

Illness, too, perhaps. But those who have done some serious inner work will come through such periods with greater courage and serenity and will continue to grow spiritually richer. Yes, if you work for the light, for a high ideal, the older you are the more expressive and alive you will be. More expressive and alive, in fact, than you ever were in your youth. Of course, you will be more bent and wrinkled and your hair will turn white, but that should not discourage you. Let your body grow old at its own rhythm and remember that the soul can still use it to manifest itself with extraordinary youthfulness. Why should we subscribe to the pessimistic attitude to old age that is so widespread in our day?

Young people are warned: 'Hurry up and make the most of your youth, because it won't last.' And that is true. It won't last. But when does this become true? It becomes true when young people listen to this pernicious advice and hasten to amuse themselves and sample every kind of pleasure while they can. In this way they soon run to seed, and – understandably, once they are less attractive and alive – others have no more use for them. Everyone sees these facts and draws their conclusions. Yes, but the facts are what they are because people are so unobservant and fail to reason correctly in the first place. What is true today (the fact that as one grows old one loses all one's strength and charm) may well not be true in the future. There, I have to give you these explanations. People must stop giving such negative advice to the young on the pretext that it is for their good.

Remember this one thing: the happiness of young people – and of old people, for that matter – lies in dedicating one's life to a high ideal. Countless human beings devote all their energies to the defence of all kinds of causes which are not really worthwhile and which, in any case, they soon abandon in favour of something else. But very few are willing to devote themselves to the service of that great ideal, the kingdom of God and his righteousness. You will say, 'The kingdom of God? But that's a Utopian dream. It will never happen.' My response to that is this: it is not our business to know whether or not it will happen. Our business is to work to make it happen. Yes, because it is the only ideal worth dedicating one's life to. It is not ours to say whether or not it will come about, but we can be quite sure of one thing, and that is that if nobody ever does anything about it because they think that their efforts are useless then, of course, it will never happen.

Chapter Nine


RISE ABOVE YOUR CIRCUMSTANCES

# I

As soon as something goes wrong, you have a tendency to blame it on unfavourable circumstances. Well, let me tell you that as long as you continue to think that your fortune or misfortune depends on circumstances, you will never be safe. Life is so arranged that nothing is ever truly stable and permanent, and this means that if you do no work with your mind and your will, you will constantly be blown hither and thither at the mercy of circumstances. You will be happy when they are in your favour and unhappy when they are not, when you meet obstacles and difficulties. And where will that lead you?

You must understand, once and for all, that the influence of circumstances is not absolute. Figs and thistles can grow in the same soil and be nourished by the same chemical elements. The children of a single family, with the same mother and father and the same upbringing, can be very different from each other physically, intellectually and morally. And we all know that the different members of a collectivity react in very different ways in the face of a common affliction. Why? Because they don't all have the same attitude in face of the same circumstances. Those who don't understand and have the wrong attitude become either bitter and vindictive or so dejected that they poison the lives of all those around them. The others, on the contrary, grow inwardly stronger and richer, and thanks to their experiences become capable of helping those around them, not only with their advice, but also by their attitude, their radiance and the forces emanating from them.

This proves that circumstances are not everything. Of course you cannot ignore them completely, but if you want to make progress, you have to realize that many things in life depend only on yourself and your own attitude, and that happiness and unhappiness are very relative states of mind. Let me give you an example of how Mullah Nashrudin, the Turkish folk-hero, proved this, for this was his philosophy, too.

One day, an old woman came to Mullah Nashrudin and complained, 'Oh Mullah, if you could see how we live. The whole family is squeezed into one tiny hut; my husband and myself, my son, his wife and their children, all in one room. It's awful! We cannot go on living like that.' 'I understand,' said the Mullah, 'And I think

I have a remedy for you.' 'What is it?' 'I'll tell you, but, first of all, you must promise to do exactly what I say without complaining.' 'Yes, yes,' said the old woman, 'I promise.' 'And you must come and see me every day and tell me how you are getting on.' 'Yes, yes: I promise.' 'All right. Now, tell me, have you got a dog?' 'Yes.' 'And a cat?' 'Yes.' 'Very well, then, tonight you must take them both into your hut for the night.' 'But Mullah,' protested the old woman, 'you don't know what you are asking.' 'You promised to do everything I told you, didn't you?' 'Yes, yes.' So the old woman went away and the cat and dog spent the night in the hut with the family. The next day, she was back again. 'It was awful,' she told the Mullah Nashrudin, 'the cat and dog did nothing but fight all night long. None of us got a wink of sleep.' 'Good! Now, have you got a goat?' 'Yes.' 'Then, tonight, you will take the goat into your hut for the night as well.' The following day she came back again: 'Oh, Mullah, it was terrible. The goat was restless all night long. She upset everything in the room and none of us got a wink of sleep.' 'Don't worry,' said the Mullah Nashrudin, 'Everything's going according to plan. Now, have you got some hens?' 'Yes, sir.' 'Then, tonight you will let them spend the night in the hut, also.' There is no need to describe the state the poor woman was in when she went back the next morning. But the Mullah

just smiled as he asked 'And have you got a pig?'
'Yes,' whispered the old woman miserably. 'Let
your pig sleep in your hut with you tonight.' She
wanted to protest, but she did not dare to break her
promise. The next morning, sobbing in despair, she
came back to see the Mullah: 'It was awful... awful!
You promised to help me, but our situation is
getting worse and worse. We are all going to go
mad. Life is hell!' 'Hmm,' murmured the Mullah
Nashrudin, tugging at his beard and looking very
grave. 'I'll tell you what you must do: let the pig
sleep outside tonight, and come back and see me
tomorrow morning.' The next day, the old woman
was all smiles. 'Oh, everything is much better. We
can breathe again, at last!' 'Good. Tonight you can
put the hens out also.' And so, one by one, all the
animals were put outside. When this was done, the
Mullah Nashrudin asked, 'Well, how are things
at home now?' 'Oh, it's extraordinary; you've no
idea how heavenly it is. The whole family is
singing and hugging each other for joy.' 'Yes,' said
the Mullah, 'And do you realize that everything is
exactly as it was the day you came and complained
that life was unbearable? So what were you
complaining about?'

Some people will say, 'What a stupid story.'
Well, I admit that it's a bit exaggerated, but it
contains an important truth, and that is that our
feelings of well-being or discomfort, happiness or

unhappiness, are all very relative. Suppose you are feeling dispirited and at a loose end, life seems drab and dull, and then, all of a sudden, you hear that there has been a terrible accident and a member of your family has been seriously injured. When you hear that you are really unhappy. But, only a few hours later, you learn that there has been a mistake; the report of an accident was not true. What joy all of a sudden! Life seems indescribably gay, beautiful and rich. Yes, but why did it not seem like that earlier? Why did you have to be told of an imaginary disaster in order to understand that you were happy before that?

Of course, I am not saying that to have to live with six or seven other people in one room is anything to be happy about. But even so, generally speaking, when you have the right philosophy and are capable of reasoning correctly, you can always do something to make yourself feel better about things, for your thoughts can influence your state of mind. This is something you must never forget: thoughts and feelings are all-powerful where consciousness is concerned. Besides, you only have to observe your own reactions; when you are suffering and feeling disgruntled with life, it is often not some material change that lightens your mood and cheers you up, but a change in your thoughts and feelings. Of course, if you are suffering physically, you will need a physical

remedy. If you have a bad cut or a broken leg, even
the very best thoughts and feelings will not heal
you or take away the pain, for they take a very long
time to reach the physical plane and make things
better. There is one thing thoughts and feelings can
do immediately, however, and that is help you to
bear the pain. Yes, for they can affect the physical
body to a certain extent; when they are harmonious
they influence the circulation and purify the blood,
and when the blood is purified, it contributes much
more effectively to the health of the whole body.
Even an open wound will heal better and more
rapidly.

As long as you have still not done the necessary
inner work, even if you do manage to improve your
material circumstances, you will soon fall back into
a state of dissatisfaction, bitterness and revolt. A
psychic need cannot be remedied on the physical
plane. You can amass everything imaginable on
the physical plane – medicines, wealth, power, etc.,
ad infinitum – but if your state of mind is not what
it should be, you will never be really satisfied. It
is in your soul and thoughts, in your point of view,
your outlook on life, your way of reasoning that
something has to change. Otherwise, however
much wealth you amass you will only be satiated
and jaded. There have been men and women who
have taken their own lives, even though, as people
said of them, 'They had everything they needed to

make them happy: youth, wealth, a loving family and many friends.' Yes, they had everything except the one thing that mattered: a love of life. None of their assets could give them that.

So it is in your heads that something must change; it is within yourselves that you must look for happiness. For once you have learned to be happy inwardly, you will always be happy, whatever the circumstances. Even in the worst possible conditions you will still be able to communicate with heavenly entities and feel yourselves fulfilled and overflowing with love. If the cause of your happiness is inside you, nothing and nobody will ever be able to take it away from you. The day you begin to see things this way will mark the beginning of liberation, immortality and eternity for you. To be sure, we all have material needs, but not nearly so many as we imagine. When fate obliges you to suffer certain privations, remind yourselves that it is an opportunity for you to seek another direction, a different path in your souls and spirits.

When the external path is closed to you, you must turn inwards – or upwards, which amounts to the same thing. There is always a way through to salvation. Sometimes, you will feel so discouraged and defeated, so annihilated, that you will even begin to envisage suicide. Yes, it can happen. I am not saying that you will find something to be happy and joyful about every day; I am simply saying that there is always something you can do about it when things go wrong – even in the most difficult cases. In fact, you must know that even in your moments of deepest discouragement, that very discouragement contains elements that could restore your courage if only you had learned to grasp and use them. For the forces contained in a state of discouragement are tremendous. Do you doubt it? Isn't the fact that it is capable of demolishing a whole kingdom – you, yourself, with all the riches and all the potential stored up in your physical body, your heart, mind, soul and spirit – enough to prove how tremendously powerful it is? So why not try to get hold of that power and use it for something constructive?

Human beings are unaware of all the possibilities that exist within them. Even when they think that they are completely burnt out and drained of every drop of energy, they still have some hidden resources, for they are built like a multiple-stage rocket; as soon as the fuel in the first stage is exhausted, the second stage is fired and the rocket continues on its course; and so on, for the second, third and fourth stages. When people die, it is not necessarily because all their resources have been used up; it is often because they has been unable to fire the next stage. If they had, they would have realized that they still had some fuel left. We are very far from imagining what immense reserves God has given us.

Try to understand what I am saying, therefore. When external paths seem to be closed to you, turn inwards and begin to work with your thought, imagination and will, and little by little you will sense that unimaginable horizons are opening up within you. If you try to understand the language of destiny, you will always be happy and grateful to heaven for leading you to discover secret regions of such wealth.

Ask any businessman who has made a fortune; do you think he will tell you that he is happy? Nothing is less certain. He will complain that he is overworked, that his wife takes advantage of his business trips to cheat on him, that his son is an idle good-for-nothing, that his workers are lazy, that his shares are falling, that he is being ruined by competitors, and so on and so forth. If you listen to him for long, you will feel as discouraged as he is. In spite of all his possessions, not only will he never be able to make you feel that life is good – for he lives in a permanent state of fear, the fear of losing all those possessions – but he will destroy your own peace of mind and *joie de vivre*. Whereas someone who has worked to acquire spiritual riches will always be ready to share those riches with you, and whatever your external circumstances, thanks to his generosity, the most effective methods and remedies to help you get your balance and discover the meaning of life will always be at your disposal.

Perhaps you feel like saying, 'But isn't it already too late for me to begin this inner work?' No; it is never too late. Naturally, the later you start the more difficult it will be, for you already have well established habits. And habits are congealed forms that, like metal, need to be softened and made malleable by fire before they can be given a new form. Well, the fire is there in the trials that the invisible world sends you in order to shape you anew and steer your life in a different direction. If your only reaction to this fire is to protest and fight against it, you prevent heaven from shaping you as it wishes, and in this case, you need not be surprised if your sufferings never end.

## II

It is not always useful to try to put something right on the physical plane, for the physical plane is the world of effects, consequences, and there is not much we can do about consequences. If you want to achieve lasting change, you have to work in the world of causes. He who is capable of entering that world through thought has the means he needs to reach and set in motion pure, luminous forces which, sooner or later, produce results. As long as your attempts to improve things are confined to the physical plane, you will never really put anything right, for you cannot prevent other people or events from coming along and, without consulting you, reorganizing things in ways that are contrary to yours. In other words, you can never be in control of the situation. To work at changing consequences is like writing on the sand of the seashore; the tide will come in and wash it all away. It is causes that have to be changed.

Conditions cannot be changed from below; the impulse has to come from above. Those who do not know this law always try to intervene on the physical plane to change things, move them about, destroy or reform them. But the lesson of history is that reforms of this kind are never conclusive: they are always followed by tides that sweep them all away.

Suppose that the rulers of a country take possession of a foreign territory and deport or murder most of the inhabitants, steal their possessions and so on. But then a few years later the situation is reversed; the conquered country rises up against the occupying power, and its tyrannical rulers or their successors find themselves faced with inextricable problems and are finally defeated. Yes, numerous examples in history show that tyrants may have a brief period of triumph but that they bequeath a disastrous heritage to their country.

Only that which is created on high, in the world of the spirit, is eternal; all the rest is transient and temporary. This is why we can say that only good is eternal; evil is necessarily ephemeral. As we say in Bulgarian: *Krivdina do pladnina, dobrina do veknina*, that is to say: 'Evil will last until tomorrow noon; good lasts for all eternity.'

When you want to improve a situation once and for all, therefore, you have to rise to a great height in the sphere of the spirit, and work there. It is on that level that you must work, pray, formulate petitions and create images that will, one day, become physical realities. One day, if you know how to set luminous forces in motion, all obstacles will be swept away and a new order of harmony and peace will reign on earth.

Chapter Ten

# DEVELOP A SENSITIVITY TO THE DIVINE

It is often said that simple, primitive, uneducated people are naturally happier than those who are highly educated, and in fact, it is true that when people's intelligence and discrimination are highly developed they become more sensitive and, therefore, more vulnerable. They are more easily affected by variations in their physical and psychological environment. So what conclusion should we draw from this? That, if we want to be happy, we must remain primitive savages? And if we believe that, why not descend even lower and live on the level of animals? Animals are happy. But perhaps plants are even happier than animals; after all, they don't suffer in the same way. And what about stones? They feel nothing. Isn't that even better? Well, there's a logical argument for you.

The principal factor that distinguishes the different realms of nature – stones, plants, animals and men – is sensitivity, the capacity to feel, for evolution is proportionate to sensitivity. Plants are more sensitive than stones; animals are more sensitive than plants, and men are more sensitive than animals. But the chain of beings does not end there; beyond man are angels, archangels and divinities. Yes, there exists a whole sequence of creatures that are more and more sensitive... all the way up to God himself. God is omniscient; he feels everything and sees everything. He knows everything because he alone is truly sensitive. These, then, are the true dimensions of sensitivity; the only truly sensitive being is God.

As for human beings, it is true that the more sensitive they become, the more vulnerable they will be and the more they will suffer. And yet it is still preferable to be sensitive, for that is what makes human beings evolve.

In order to have a clear understanding of this question, we need to refer to the notion of the two natures that co-exist within us, our lower and our higher nature. Of course, as long as someone has never seriously worked to control the egocentric tendencies of his lower nature, his growth in sensitivity is bound to be accompanied by difficulties and suffering of all kinds. And unfortunately the instruction given in our schools and universities only makes things worse; by emphasizing the acquisition of knowledge rather than the formation of character, education provides young people with an excuse to be more and more selfish, discontented and demanding. No attempt is ever made to teach students to use the knowledge they receive for a nobler, more generous purpose. On the contrary. Whatever their area of specialization, they all learn to use their knowledge in order to promote their social standing and prestige and their material well-being. And when they become adults and have responsibilities in society, since their one thought is to get as large a slice of the cake as possible, they are always dissatisfied and aggressive, always ready to quarrel and take offence. They feel constantly threatened by the egocentric behaviour of others, fearing that they will be deprived of what they consider to be their due.

This neurotic sensitivity that is nourished by the lower nature, the personality, makes life so impossible that people conclude that if they want to be happy, they had better not be sensitive.

In reality, it is important to distinguish between true sensitivity and this unhealthy, thin-skinned attitude that should, more accurately, be called touchiness or hypersensitivity. True sensitivity is a faculty that enables us to travel very high and very far, and to perceive and grasp the realities of ever subtler worlds. Hypersensitivity, on the other hand, is a manifestation of the lower nature which, because it takes itself for the centre of the world, feels frustrated and hurt when others show a lack of consideration, and consequently responds aggressively. Once this distinction becomes clear, it is easy to see that a great deal of work needs to be done in order to subdue and control our lower nature. This is the only way to allow our true sensitivity to develop and become richer.

Sensitivity is more than a faculty that allows us to be moved to a sense of wonder by those we love or by the beauty of nature or works of art. It is also a faculty that opens our eyes to immensity and light, that gives us an understanding of the divine order of things and makes it possible for us to vibrate in unison with heavenly regions, entities and currents.

This is the sensitivity that all human beings must cultivate if mankind is not to regress. So many people today give the impression that they are reverting to the level of animals, vegetables or even stones. They make no effort to cultivate their sensitivity; they let themselves go completely, and when man lets himself go, he necessarily regresses. When, on the contrary, we cultivate true sensitivity, our matter becomes subtler, finer and purer, and vibrates differently. At the same time that this true sensitivity opens our eyes to the divine world, it closes them to stupidity, wickedness and insults; we become indifferent to them. Before developing this higher sensitivity, we reacted to the slightest sign of hostility, whereas, now, we no longer even notice. It is this true sensitivity, the sensitivity of the soul and spirit, that protects us from that sickly, ridiculous hypersensitivity that is a product of our lower nature. It has a twofold advantage, therefore: it opens us to light, beauty and the bliss of the divine world, and it protects us from the darkness, ugliness and sufferings of earth. This is something that deserves considerable reflection.

Now, if you want to develop this sensitivity to the divine world, it is also very important that you become increasingly aware of the value of certain moments of your existence, of those special moments of silence and inner recollection in which you receive a light, a grace from heaven. Much of your suffering comes precisely from the fact that you do not have this awareness. You receive all kinds of blessings, but they don't last, they soon evaporate simply because you are not aware of the value of what you receive. There is always something else which seems more important to you... some odd job that has to be done, some insignificant trifle that you want to discuss. You imagine that heaven should always be there, ready to pour down its blessings on you when you feel like it, when you have nothing more interesting to do and are willing to sit still for a few minutes to receive them. No, that is not the way it should be. Heaven is not at the beck and call of heedless, superficial human beings. At certain moments and

given certain conditions, it will pour out its
blessings, and if you are not sufficiently conscious
to receive them or if you don't know how to hold
on to them, it will be your loss, for they will slip
away from you.

Pay attention to this question, therefore. When
you feel that you have received a grace, a revelation
from heaven, try to cherish it and not let it go. In
fact, I have given you a method for this. You can
try to remember the most luminous moments of
your life and see who or what caused them, and
when you have done this once, you can conjure
them up in your mind often, just as you often play
a recording of a favourite piece of music. In this
way, you can live the same sensations of purity,
freedom and light over and over again.

Unfortunately, most people do just the opposite.
The memories they most often conjure up are of
things that have made them suffer. They keep
holding on to them, looking at them and ruminating
on them. And this is very dangerous; you must not
keep reverting to negative things. You must draw
whatever conclusion needs to be drawn from them
once and for all, and then leave them strictly alone.
You do yourselves a lot of harm by continually
harping on negative events or states of mind.

Henceforth, therefore, when God gives you his
blessings, treasure them with the utmost care, for
happiness lies in a constant attention to what is

beautiful, in a sensitivity to all that is divine. When you feel that you have been visited by the spirit, by light, don't let the impression be wiped out by immediately thinking of other things; dwell on it for as long as possible so that it may soak deep into your being and produce results. In this way, it will leave traces within you for all eternity. But it is a habit that has to be deliberately cultivated: instead of nourishing and reinforcing negative states of mind, disappointments or animosities by constantly dwelling on them, leave them alone, shrug them off, and concentrate on all the good, pure, luminous things that have happened to you.

Chapter Eleven

# THE LAND OF CANAAN

As soon as you realize that you have lost your way, that you have been working for negative forces by allowing yourselves to be tempted by some insignificant, fleeting pleasures, turn back immediately and put as much distance as possible between yourselves and the dangerous regions in which you first went astray. You must understand that everything depends on the regions in which you choose to linger. If you venture below a certain borderline – let's say, symbolically, below the cloud level – you will necessarily come under the rulership of the clouds, and will be cold and in darkness. But if you rise above the level of the clouds, you will find yourselves bathed in light and warmth. As you see, it all depends on you.

Religion teaches that God punishes us for our evil deeds and rewards us for our good deeds. This is simply one way of presenting things. The truth is that God neither punishes nor rewards us. It is we ourselves who, by our thoughts, feelings and acts, choose to dwell in this or that region, with the result that we either suffer or benefit from the conditions that prevail in the region of our choice. And it is not at all the same thing to choose the regions of light or the regions of darkness.

'That which is below is like that which is above,' said Hermes Trismegistus. And this means, also, that that which is external is like that which is internal; that which is outside is like that which is inside. You will find all kinds of different regions on earth; some of them are wooded, fertile and full of flowers, and you can wander in them and admire them in complete safety. Others are wildernesses, swamps or jungles infested with man-eating beasts and poisonous reptiles in which danger surrounds you on all sides. Yes, there is a little of everything in the world: tumultuous torrents and smooth, calm lakes; lofty peaks and deep canyons; volcanoes and glaciers. You know all this, of course, but what you don't know is that these same regions exist within you. Within you, too, there are peaks and precipices, swamps and flower-gardens, deserts and fertile plains.

It is good to be versed in geography, geology and agriculture, but it is even more important to be familiar with the regions that exist within oneself and to learn how to stay away from some and to dwell in others so as to care for and cultivate them. It is good to know how to sail on the rivers and oceans of the world or to climb its mountains, but it is even better to know how to control one's inner storms and whirlwinds and to climb to the peak of spiritual mountains. So, this is the work that is waiting for you: to explore the different regions that exist within you, and by means of thought, meditation, prayer and contemplation, reach the Promised Land spoken of in Genesis, the land of Canaan, the land 'flowing with milk and honey,' symbols of the full and perfect life.

Man's life is one long voyage of exploration in search of new and unknown lands. Some of the lands he reaches are friendly and hospitable and he can rest in them for a while; others are unfriendly and dangerous and he should avoid them or, if he has been so rash as to set foot in them, he should flee from them as quickly as possible. Many poets and philosophers have compared life to a journey, and now you can see why. Even if you spend your whole life at home, even if you never move out of your room, you can discover within yourself every phenomenon and every landscape that exists in nature. There are days when you complain, 'I don't know what's the matter with me; I feel as though I were suffocating!' and the answer is that you are so far underground that you feel crushed by a great weight. All you have to do to be free is to go up again into the fresh air. Then you will say, 'Ah, I feel lighter. I can breathe freely at last.' Then there are days, on the contrary, when you feel weightless and inspired as though you were no longer bound by the laws of gravity, and this always means that you have climbed up to a mountain top – whether you did so consciously or not.

It is also possible – although it is extremely rare and can only occur in exceptional conditions – for this experience of weightlessness to be physical, to walk as though you were flying. One day, during my first visit to India, I was in Kashmir, up in the region of Gulmarg, beyond Srinagar. I was walking in the mountains and contemplating the magnificent spectacle of Nanga Parbat, one of the highest peaks of the Himalayas. All of a sudden I felt as though I were being borne aloft; I moved so effortlessly, it was as though my feet no longer touched the ground; I climbed up those slopes as though I were flying. This happened to me only once in my life and the memory of it will always be with me.

Chapter Twelve

# THE SPIRIT IS ABOVE THE LAWS OF FATE

All the trials we experience in life are sent to us for a reason, and you have to try to find that reason. If you search for it because you sincerely want to make progress, the Invisible world will give you the answers you are seeking, for it is not cruel and implacable. It may even show you in what way you broke the divine laws in a previous incarnation, and how the trials you experience today have been sent to persuade you to make reparation for your mistakes and are in accordance with a higher justice. Of course you will say, 'But why does justice have to take this form? Couldn't it be done more kindly and gently? Why can't it pet and console me and explain lovingly just what I should do in order to reform? I'm not completely stupid; I would understand.'

Unfortunately, you don't really know yourself. Heavenly entities have already tried, time and again and in every way possible, to convince you that you should be more conscientious, more honest and patient, more generous, etc., but you have never heard or seen or understood them. That is why, today, since you have proved to be so deaf and blind and stubborn in the past, you need to be shaken up a bit, you need to be burned and bitten a little; you need to be prodded. It is for this reason that divine justice has sent you to incarnate in difficult circumstances that will oblige you to suffer and to pay your debts and learn a certain number of truths. And you must accept the situation.

In any case, even if you refuse to accept it, that won't change anything. Nobody can escape or find a way round the decrees of divine justice. This is why it is useless to go and consult astrologers, as many people do, in the hope that they can warn you of accidents or disasters that may threaten you. It is useless to try to hide from fate. However many precautions you take, you cannot avoid anything. You cannot trick fate into letting you off. The only thing you can do is work with light so that, when the days of tribulation come, you will be better prepared to put up with it.

Suppose that you know, for example, that you are going to be seriously ill; by living wisely and purifying and strengthening your organism, you can arm yourself for the battle with that illness. You will not be able to avoid it altogether, but you will be in a position to limit the amount of damage it does. This law applies in every domain. Your efforts to reinforce and purify yourself will always put you in a better position to face up to your trials.

Destiny cannot be moved to pity, but it is never cruel; it is simply just. All the faults you have committed are piled up on one side of the scales, but if you decide to amend your life the good things you do will add weight to the other side of the scales. In this way, when the time comes to pay for your transgressions, your good thoughts, sentiments and actions will be taken into account and your debt will be lighter. This means also that you must not become fatalistic and say, 'Since my fate is thus and so, there is nothing I can do about it. I just have to accept it.' No; there is one thing you must never forget, and it is this: fate never wants to stifle or extinguish the spirit. On the contrary, its role is to oblige us to awaken the spirit, to work with the spirit in order to create a new destiny for ourselves.

Because of the faults committed in previous incarnations, man is now subject to fate. The Hindus say that he has to pay his karma. But this does not mean that there is nothing he can do about it; if he simply lies down under it he will end by being totally crushed. On the contrary, he must fight with weapons of love and light so as to triumph over his fate and come under the rule of providence. And once there, fate no longer has a hold on him, because he dwells in the realm of light. He moves onto another plane where the laws are no longer the same; he leaves the world of fate and enters the world of grace.

Most people have very vague ideas on the subject; they often think that everything that happens to them in life, good or bad, is fate. No, the word 'fate' should be used to refer to what happens as a result of your ignorance or your faults, whereas what happens to you as a result of your light and all the good things you have done is providence. So, now this is clear: providence is always there for those who dwell in the light and in divine love, and fate is the lot of those who persist in their blindness and wickedness.

Someone who wants to escape from the dominion of fate must begin by seeing things with lucidity; he must recognize which of his thoughts, sentiments and acts continue to add to the weight of his karma, and make a real effort to behave reasonably and become purer and more disinterested. In this way, he can enter the realm of providence and start to create his true future.

With a few extremely rare exceptions, no human being has ever been born into this world without some faults for which he has to make reparation or some debts to pay.

Even many Initiates, Saints and Prophets have had to suffer in order to make reparation for faults committed in previous incarnations. But this did not prevent their souls and spirits from dwelling in divine splendour. Yes, because they worked, worked unceasingly, in spite of their karma, and became divinities.

Whatever happens to you, you must always bear in mind that there is this one impregnable, invulnerable region within you, your spirit. It is in this region that you must take refuge in order to work. If you do this, even though your karma may rage all about you, you will feel that you are above it, always above it. Your karma tries to shackle you, but you free yourself; it tries to drag you into darkness, but you switch on all your lights, for in the teeth of every obstacle you go on working. Yes, you must always try to reach this place that is beyond and above the regions subject to karma.

The great question, now, is to see whether you can climb up there, whether you are capable of going and settling in this region that is beyond the reach of winds, tornadoes and lightning. It was this region that Jesus was talking about when he said that the wise man 'builds his house on the rock.' The rock is this region of the spirit which must be our permanent home, because it is the only place that is not at the mercy of wind and weather. It is also the 'shelter of the Most High' spoken of in Psalm 91: the causal plane. Until such time as you have reached this region by means of thought and meditation, you will continue to stagnate in the lower regions of the mental and astral planes, and in those regions you will always be vulnerable, a prey to every kind of torment.

I hope that these few words will make the question clearer to you. You cannot dodge your karma; nobody can, but you can pay it off in many different ways. In everyday life also, although you pay for most things with money, there are others ways of settling a debt. You can work, for instance, or give your creditor a present or make yourself useful to him in some way. Similarly, the best way to pay off a spiritual debt is to amass a great deal of gold, by which I mean to cultivate qualities and virtues. But prayer, too, is a form of payment, for you put gold into your prayer; all that is best in your heart and soul and spirit goes into your prayer; you regret your faults and promise to make reparation for them by your good deeds. Then heaven says, 'Since he repents and wants to make reparation, it means that he has understood. Let us make his trials lighter.' Yes, for what does heaven want? It wants us to reform. It is not interested in crushing us completely; what would it gain from that? Its only desire is that we should become wiser and more fully conscious. This is why, if we continue to resist, it has to send us trials and tribulations, but if it sees that we understand without having to suffer all those trials, it is perfectly satisfied; it has no desire to wipe us out.

There are many examples in the past of people who have paid off their karmic debts by working for others, by sacrificing themselves, by giving their time and strength, their thoughts, their souls. For it is not because we know that the law of karma exists that we should use it as a pretext for indifference to the sufferings of other human beings. Unfortunately, I have seen this happen: once they learn about karma, instead of thinking with compassion of those who suffer and making up their minds to do something to help them, some so-called spiritual people are content to do nothing, saying, 'It's their karma.' Well, if it is to become just one more reason for people to remain prisoners of their own selfishness, it would sometimes be better if they never heard about karma. This is why I consider that the fact that Westerners cannot see other people suffering without wanting to do something about it is a very real superiority. Whenever there is a disaster somewhere – famine, an epidemic, a flood or an earthquake – they organize help, and this is magnificent.

Actually, of course, it would be better if everyone knew the laws of destiny and understood why certain misfortunes happen to them and to others, but without ceasing to try to help them. Some people might ask, 'But why should we help them if they are only getting what they deserve?' You should help them, first of all, because the efforts we make to help others are never wasted. In some circumstances, seeing the sincerity with which you try to help, heaven will relent. And then, too, your efforts benefit you, for by helping others you advance and develop certain qualities in yourself. This is what I always tell people who ask me why I give so much of my time to trying to help others: 'Because I can feel that it does me good, that it has a good effect on me.' And what about you? Why shouldn't you do as much? You would feel so much better for it.

As to whether those you try to help will actually benefit and be saved by what you do for them – only God knows the answer. I am not so naïve as to think that it is easy to be useful to others. I often say to myself, 'Poor old man, you think that just because you have spent hours and hours listening to people talking about their problems and sufferings, and trying to console them and give them good advice, that they are going to be guided by what you say and start putting their lives straight. Don't delude yourself. Most of them will continue, for a long time to come, to go wherever anyone else pushes them. But you must still continue to do what you can for them, because this is how you yourself gain in strength and light. If they don't want to work for the coming of the kingdom of God, that need not prevent you from doing so. The kingdom of God will come, if only to you.'

How wonderful it would be if everybody could be as 'egotistical' as this. Yes, we must be egoists; we must think of ourselves. 'Now you're contradicting yourself,' you will say; 'You are always telling us to be disinterested, and now you say just the opposite.' Yes, because the truth is that absolute disinterestedness doesn't exist. What exists are different kinds or levels of self-interest: there is a gross, lower, material self-interest, and then there is a higher, sublime, divine self-interest. The only question of real importance for you, therefore, is to know where your own best interest lies. Someone who believes that his best interest lies, first and foremost, in organizing his worldly affairs, in becoming rich, powerful and glorious in men's eyes, should know that when he gets to the next world, he will be naked, poor, woeful, ugly and deformed. And this shows that he doesn't know where his best interest lies.

And this applies to you, too. Try to understand how important it is for you to work for the good of all. This is how you can pay off your karma. Some people say, 'Ha, I'm not going to be so stupid. I'm not going to do anything for others. I'm going to make the most of life. I'm going to "eat, drink and be merry".' Well, anyone who says this will, sooner or later, in one form or another, feel the full weight of his karma on his shoulders. He may think that he is very clever but, in fact, he is just stupid and ignorant.

This is why initiatic science is so useful: because it teaches us to abide by these rules and laws and methods so that we may, eventually, be free, strong and happy. Anyone who neglects this science is working against his own best interest.

When you have to endure trials, therefore, instead of complaining and feeling sorry for yourselves, reflect on your situation calmly and ask yourselves, 'What do heaven and all my heavenly friends have in mind for me? What is it they want me to get out of this?' If you do this you will be given light and will understand what they want you to learn; whether it is to be more patient or less vulnerable or more intelligent, and so on. In this way, not only will you no longer rebel against your trials, but you will learn to be grateful and to give thanks for them. Not only that, but the virtues that heaven is urging you to acquire will come to you more readily.

One often hears people saying that it was thanks to an accident, a serious illness or some great affliction that they found their true vocation – or even their salvation. And yet to start with they had been defiant and in despair, because they believed that it was the end of everything for them. To be sure, some of the trials we have to endure are terrible, it is impossible not to suffer. But why not think, at once, about the happiness that is waiting for you once your trials are over? Why waste so much time in thoughts of despair and revolt?

Whatever their trials, Initiates continue their work, continue to dwell in light and love, because they understand that this is the only thing that matters. Be glad that you have this teaching, therefore; be glad and thankful for all these gems, for the immense potential that it reveals within you and within your spirit for a work of gigantic proportions. What would become of you if you did not have this light?

Chapter Thirteen

# LOOK FOR HAPPINESS
# ON A HIGHER LEVEL

The most dangerous thing human beings can do is to adopt a materialistic philosophy that drives them to seek every satisfaction on the physical plane, for in doing so, they become selfish, unjust, dishonest and ready to resort to crime. For the sake of a salary increase, a more prestigious post, a bigger share of the market or an invitation to a fashionable reception, they are ready for every kind of underhand scheme or dishonourable compromise. But what do they actually gain when they manage to achieve their goal? Very often, as soon as they have got what they wanted, they begin to feel dissatisfied again. They have injured others all for nothing, for they are no happier than they were before. In short, none of this is very profitable.

He who seeks happiness in material things is like a man who sifts through tons of sand in the hope of finding a speck of gold-dust. That is not a very profitable enterprise either. If you want to find masses of gold, you have to rise to a great height, to the level of the sun, the level of the spirit. Down below you will find only refuse, husks, dross.

To be sure, we cannot uproot ourselves from matter. We have a physical body and this physical body serves as the intermediary by means of which we relate to everything around us; and this is just as well, for if we ceased to relate to our surroundings we would die. So we need to eat, drink and sleep, to have clothes and a roof over our heads, to work, recreate and love, and so on. But do we really have to devote so much time and effort to these things? One day we shall be tired of all that.

What should we do to avoid becoming tired and jaded? Let me give you an example in the area of food. For years I have been telling you that it is good to learn to eat in silence and with love and gratitude. Why? Because this attitude puts you in touch with the subtle dimension of your food, and it is these subtle, imperceptible elements that contribute far more to your health and equilibrium than the quantity you eat. And not only do they give you health and equilibrium, but they also transform something within the very quintessence of your being; your heart becomes more generous and your thoughts more lucid. This is what I mean by 'looking for happiness on a higher level;' it means adding elements of a spiritual nature to all your material activities.

And the same can be said of love. Just as human beings cannot nourish themselves without absorbing solid, material food, nor can they – apart from some very rare exceptions – love without feeling a need for the exchange of endearments on the physical level. But this does not mean that they have to wallow in sensuality, day and night. Methods exist in this area also. In fact, I have already given you a great deal of advice about how to raise your intercourse to the subtler planes. At the moment, of course, you still consider these things to be nothing more than preliminaries. Your experiments in this area are only partially successful; you have glimpsed certain possibilities but you have not achieved anything conclusive. And that is normal. It is almost impossible to achieve total success, for that is the crowning point of initiation, but you must never renounce your efforts to find joy and happiness on a much higher plane. There is no law that forbids you to use all that cosmic intelligence has put at your disposal, on the contrary; but you must always try to use it in order to reach further heights of purity and light.

This question of man's relationship with matter should be clear to you now. Our descent into matter is neither a mistake nor simply accidental to the course of our evolution. It was specifically planned by cosmic intelligence. In order to attain the fullness of knowledge, human beings needed to develop their intellectual faculties, and this could only be achieved if they were placed in conditions which dimmed their perception of the invisible world and encouraged them to explore the dimension of matter. This is why mankind is still at this phase of his evolution. But it is not the final phase. Mankind still has to return to the regions of the soul and spirit that it knew before, and when it does so, it will take with it all the wealth that the intellect has enabled it to gain from its experience in the realm of matter.

At the moment, we are witnessing the dizzying descent of human consciousness into the depths of matter. And as the wealth and diversity of matter is inexhaustible there is never any limit to what men can see and touch and amass. This is why they end by forgetting what they are and losing themselves in matter. But, although matter is inexhaustible, what it gives can satisfy only men's physical needs, and the day will come when they feel glutted and surfeited and long to return to the higher regions of the spirit. New needs will begin to awaken within them, for once they have touched and tasted and possessed all that the physical plane has to offer, they will sense that this is not where true happiness lies for them.

In the meantime, everything in our environment today is designed to encourage our desire to immerse ourselves in matter. You only have to look at the publicity that is continually trying to persuade people that such and such a skin-cream, washing machine, brand of coffee, perfume, piece of jewellery or car can transform their lives. And they all rush out and buy these things. Ah, if only it were so easy to transform one's life! I don't deny that all these products and machines are both useful and agreeable, but they cannot give us anything really substantial. This is proved by the fact that even when people possess them – and many other things besides – they still feel a void in their life.

One day, a new philosophy will come – a new philosophy which is, in reality, the eternal philosophy of the Initiates – and it will show human beings that it is by turning back to the higher planes that they will recover the wealth they were obliged to leave behind when they began to descend into matter. And not only will they recover this wealth but, thanks to a higher degree of comprehension, they will also benefit to the full from all that they have acquired on the physical plane where there is so much to be studied, worked with and enjoyed. The knowledge of matter, therefore, was an integral part of the programme designed by cosmic intelligence for man's evolution. But to know matter does not mean to bury oneself in it. You must understand, henceforth, that if you want to find happiness, you must constantly move higher and settle down – with all your furniture, your refrigerator, your clothes, your records, your armchairs and your cars – on that higher level. Well, that is a figure of speech, because I don't think that you could really get very high if you burdened yourselves with all that stuff. I simply mean that you must always remember to transform whatever you are doing by adding a spiritual element.

Chapter Fourteen


# THE QUEST FOR HAPPINESS
# IS A QUEST FOR GOD

Happiness is like a ball: you keep running after it, and just as you are about to catch up with it, you give it a good kick... and start running after it all over again. For it is the chase that stimulates you. It is in the pursuit, in the drive towards your goal that you find happiness. When you long for something, therefore, don't be in too much of a hurry to satisfy your longing, for that is what buoys you up and keeps you on your toes. Knowing this law, I keep all the longings that I know I can never fulfil hidden away in my soul and spirit, and it is they that keep me alive.

Yes, this is the great secret. Why ask for something that can be had in a few months or years? It's too easy. You will never be happy if your goal is so close to hand that you can obtain it without having recourse to the divine, inexhaustible fountainhead, for only this fountainhead can give you everything your heart desires. When you get what you wanted, of course, you will be happy for a little while, but that satisfaction is almost immediately followed by a feeling of emptiness; you have to start looking for something else and you are never satisfied. So what is the solution? To start looking for the farthest and most inaccessible goal: perfection, immensity and eternity. And, on the way, you will find everything else: knowledge, wealth, power and love. Yes, you will win these things without even having to ask for them, whereas if you set your heart on just one of them, you will be limiting yourself to that one thing and all the rest will pass you by. In fact, the Lord alone knows whether you will get even that one thing.

This is why the very best advice I can give you is this: never ask for anything but the unattainable, the impossible. In this way, you will find everything else along the way, without having to waste time going to look for it. Yes, but how many people think as I do about this? People are always thinking to themselves, 'Ah, if only I can get that job, or win that award, or marry that girl, or have children, etc., I shall be happy.' But even when they get these things nothing much changes; they are still unhappy because, instead of fixing their sights on a distant goal that would oblige them to keep moving forward, their aspirations stopped there.

Besides, it is God himself who planted feelings of dissatisfaction and emptiness in the souls of his creatures, and that emptiness will only be filled when they are finally one with him. As long as men still have not achieved this union, they will continue to search and experiment with different solutions, thinking each time that they are about to find what they were looking for; and each time they will be disappointed and disillusioned. Actually, this disappointment is not such a bad thing, for it drives men to go on and on searching.

God is everywhere in the universe; he is hidden in all the things that our hearts long for. In their own way, the ambitious, the drunkards, gluttons, misers and lechers are all seeking God, for, in fact, a tiny particle of God can be found even in alcohol, food, sexuality, money, glory and power. Yes, you can find God in everything, even in the middle of a swamp, even in a stone, in which his presence is buried like a minute spark of fire. But of course the satisfaction to be gained from these things is only momentary, for God cannot be found in any real way in the lowest forms and the densest layers of matter.

All human beings without exception seek God, but without knowing that it is God they are looking for. They believe that they are only looking for happiness. Who doesn't look for happiness? Everyone wants to be happy; it is the only thing they want in fact, but they always imagine that it will take a particular form. You only have to observe human beings to see the extraordinary variety of forms in which they expect to find happiness, forms which are very often in direct contradiction with each other. Some find happiness in study and reflection, others in light-heartedness and amusements. Some need a family life, while others prefer celibacy and solitude. Some seek opulence, comfort and glory, while others seek austerity, asceticism and anonymity. Some aspire to a lively, adventurous life and others to a peaceful, uneventful existence. Some need to help their neighbour, to succour and care for others, and some need to persecute and destroy them.

Each individual seeks happiness in his own way, depending on his own particular temperament, and however different these ways may be, they are always a form of the quest for God – a quest that may show a lack of wisdom or a lack of light perhaps, but which is still a quest for God. Yes, because God is hidden behind this notion of happiness. It is he who gave men this aspiration for happiness, so that in pursuing it they would eventually reach him. And even if, in the meantime, they seek God in ways that lead through chimneys, sewers, swamps or graveyards, in the long run, after a multitude of experiences, they will understand that they have to seek him in the highest regions, in the form of purity and light. And there, at last, they will find him.

All human beings are destined to find God, one day, in this sublime form, but before they can find him they must, at least, love him. It is not God who needs our love. If the great Masters of all religions have taught the love of God, it is because they were familiar with the law of magic that corresponds in the spiritual world to a phenomenon that we witness every day in the physical world. When you throw a ball against a wall, the wall sends it back to you. When you throw words against a cliff, the echo of your words bounces back at you. Similarly, when you send your love to God, you set the same law in motion and oblige divine love to be reflected back to you. God does not need us, but we need God; and the only way to draw him to us is by loving him.

If you want to receive, you have to give. If you don't hold out your glass to me, I cannot fill it with water. If you don't hold out your heart to God, he cannot fill it with his blessings. If we want to receive the strength, light, wisdom and beauty of God, the fullness of God, we have to give him our love. It is this love that triggers, in return, the flood of divine grace into our hearts.

Chapter Fifteen


NO HAPPINESS FOR EGOISTS

It is not by being egotistical that you will best defend your interests. On the contrary, it is in your interest to think of others because, by doing so, you improve the conditions of your own existence. Let me illustrate this: you are walking down a path one day when you come across a lot of broken glass and you leave it there, thinking, 'After all, it's not my fault if it's there. Somebody else can sweep it up.' And then, later that night, fate sends you home by the same path. You have forgotten about the glass, and in the dark, you step on it and cut yourself. Then, of course, you exclaim, 'Who was the idiot who left broken glass on a public footpath? What a criminal thing to do.' Yes, but it is too late to ask yourself that; you should have swept it up the first time you went by.

Those who never think about others believe that they are being very intelligent. The only trouble is that something always happens to them that they had not foreseen... which only goes to

show that they are not as intelligent as all that. For
intelligence is also the capacity to look into the
future and foresee the consequences of one's acts
– or of one's failure to act. When you fail to do
what is good for others, you always store up a lot
of trouble for your own future.

To refuse to think of others is not only a lack
of love, therefore; it is also a lack of intelligence.
And that is not all. When you have neither enough
love to feel what you should do for others nor
enough intelligence to see it, you leave all kinds
of loose ends lying about and do nothing to remedy
the situation; and this denotes a lack of will-power.
Look at the thing for yourselves. When three things
of such primary importance as the intelligence that
foresees consequences, the love that urges you to
try to improve things and the will-power that is
capable of facing up to difficulties… when all these
things are lacking, what success can you possibly
hope for in life?

The extraordinary thing is that it is people like
this who are always the first to complain that they
lack this, that somebody owes them that, that
nobody loves them or thinks of them, that
everybody is against them, and so on. Why can
they never understand that it is their own
selfishness and unreasonable demands that put
other people off? They need to be helped and
encouraged. Yes, no doubt, but they would do well

to start by thinking a little less about their own needs and a little more about the needs of others. They will never be happy if they allow themselves to be dictated to by their own selfishness.

All those who take themselves for the centre of the universe, who always want the biggest slice of the cake, who imagine that everyone else should orbit around them, serve them and grovel before them as though they were princes and princesses... all those who have this attitude are preparing a future of frustration and misery for themselves. If you want to be happy, you have to become a servant.

Would it really be asking too much of you to beg you, once again, to expand your consciousness, to open your eyes to broader horizons? Try to forget about all the things you have not got. How can you possibly feel lonely, defenceless and humiliated when your thought has the power to embrace the entire universe and put you in touch with all the luminous entities that inhabit it? What more do you need in order to understand that you are rich, that you have everything, that you are in a position to help others? Learn to be generous; share your wealth, even your material wealth if you possibly can, otherwise your fear of losing it will always be uppermost in your minds, and in the long run you will simply forget that there are others who are wretched and in need. Go ahead! Share it out! In this way you will no longer go in fear and trembling of being robbed, and at the same time, your gesture will be recorded in heaven, and one day, it will be returned to you a hundred-fold. But how can one get human beings to understand this? They are so selfish and avaricious; they want everything for themselves. It never occurs to them to try to make other people happy, and that is why they are never happy themselves.

You cannot be happy if your field of vision is too narrow. This is why there is no happiness for egoists, because egoists are all shrunken and shrivelled up. If you want to be happy you have to open up and take the whole world into your embrace, and love is the only thing that makes this possible. Those who have a great deal of love grow and expand; they embrace the whole universe and vibrate in unison with it; everything lies open before them; there are no more obstacles or barriers to hold them up; they are in a permanent state of happiness. The road to happiness is the road of love. Yes, neither knowledge nor philosophy, only love. Knowledge and learning cannot give us happiness; they can prepare the way, guide us and enlighten us, but they cannot make us happy. Solomon showed that he understood this when he said, 'In much wisdom is much grief, and he who increases knowledge increases sorrow.' Those who have a lot of knowledge are not happy, whereas those who have a lot of heart, even if they don't know much, are far happier. Why? Because God gave the gift of happiness to the heart and not to the intellect. But the heart must be generous, of course; heaven and earth have sworn never to give happiness to a selfish heart. You will say, 'But we all know plenty of people who never work for anyone but themselves. The only thing they are interested in is becoming rich, powerful and famous, and yet they are happy.' Yes, they may seem to be perfectly happy, but how long will it last? That is what you have to consider. Their devious schemes may get them all the material things they want, but in reality they will be deprived of the only things that are essential: peace, joy and fulfilment. Even if they are deprived of nothing on the physical plane, they will inevitably feel inwardly deprived.

Heaven wants to know whom you serve, and if it sees that you serve your own god, your egoism, your own lower nature, it turns away from you. It does not distribute its riches to people who are only interested in their own corrupt, pleasure-seeking, animal way of life. And when heaven turns away from you, who is going to help you? Who can save you? Your money? Your glory? Your fame? Heaven sees only two categories of beings: those who work exclusively for their own selfish interests, for the gratification of their own appetites, and those who make an effort to help their fellow human beings and participate in the work of the billions and billions of entities in the invisible world who are working for the coming of the kingdom of God on earth. And it is these whose names are inscribed with all the other benefactors of mankind in the great book of life.

Chapter Sixteen

# GIVE WITHOUT EXPECTING ANYTHING IN RETURN

When someone does something for others, when he helps and supports them, he thinks it only normal that they should show their gratitude, or at least give some sign of appreciation. Those who have devoted themselves to their children, for instance, who have nourished and educated them, expect them to acknowledge, at the very least, that they have been good parents. And here am I, about to demolish this way of looking at things – which has been considered normal and legitimate from the beginning of the world – by telling them that they should expect nothing at all.

Some of you will probably feel like asking, 'Why does he say such peculiar things?' The reason is very simple: when you expect approval or gratitude, you are entering the world of dissatisfaction, recriminations, bitterness and mental torment. You will say, 'Does this mean that the good we do will never be recognized?' No, it will be recognized, but you must not expect or wait for it to be recognized. All Initiates and sages know one great law on which they base their lives: the law of cause and effect. They know that, sooner or later, everything they do will come back to them. If what they do is good, the effects will be beneficial; and if it is bad... This is the law on which the wise base their lives, and you should do the same.

What does anyone know about reality? Sometimes, one even wonders whether the world itself really exists. In fact, there have been philosophers who claimed that there was no such thing as objective reality, that the reality we perceived was simply the effect of our personal, subjective impressions. I remember that, when I was very young, I read some of these philosophers – people such as Berkeley or Ernst Mach – and although I was astounded by their arguments I must say that I found them very convincing. Many things can be doubted, therefore, but there is one law that the Initiates never doubt, and that is that we always reap what we have sown, and that if we sow good seed, we can be sure that, sooner or later, we shall reap good fruits.

There is a form of yoga in India called 'Karma-yoga,' and its adepts train themselves to act without expecting to gain any benefit from their actions. For it is in this way that man grows and becomes nobler, stronger and more powerful and comes closer to the Deity. But the spirit of Karma-yoga is completely alien to Westerners. When Westerners give something they always expect some kind of reward.

And then there is something else that you have to understand, and that is that the laws of the cosmos are not in a hurry as we are; they march to another rhythm. This is why our rewards (and our punishments, too, for that matter) are always rather slow in coming, and if you get impatient or angry, you will only complicate things. Why suffer and torment yourselves? Sooner or later your reward will come, and knowing this, you can be completely detached and carefree. This is why you must never expect or wait for anything. You can be quite certain that you will be rewarded one day, that gifts are already on their way. If you are bitter and angry, it only shows that you do not possess this true knowledge.

You are in an initiatic school in order to learn truths without which you would be condemned to struggle helplessly in an endless series of problems. These truths will enable you to clear away all the debris that clutters your path, so that you may continue to advance.

In fact, let me tell you something else: you must learn to do something for others without even letting them know that it was you who did it. In this way, you awaken something good in response, for they will be obliged to wonder who their magnificent, unknown benefactor is, and will be encouraged to do things for others in the same way. Of course, this applies to me, too. I should be able to give you this teaching without your knowing that it is I who am giving it. But how can I? I can't hide when I am talking to you; you can see that the words are coming from me. But I would far rather that these words were silent so that you would not know that it is I who explain things to you. Actually, I often do exactly this when I am alone at home, or in the silence during the meditations. For I know all your problems and anxieties, and even when I cannot see you, I continue to give you explanations and advice. I can even reveal certain things to you that I could never reveal in words. But it is up to you to be attentive and to look for occasional enlightenment and illumination within yourselves. Even if you do not know that it was I who gave you that illumination, try to find and make use of it.

Those who are capable of giving without revealing themselves as the giver evolve magnificently and experience a secret joy that those who hasten to say, 'It was I who sent you that,' can never experience. The fact that they announce their good deeds aloud shows that they expect to be rewarded, and as our rewards are sometimes a very long time in coming, they become angry, impatient and miserable at being obliged to wait.

What is more marvellous than to love other human beings without asking for anything in return; to enlighten and purify them and guide them towards the light? But you must do it naturally, just as the sun shines in the sky and the flowers fill the air with their scent without expecting to be rewarded for it. Yes, think of all the flowers that grow high up in the mountains and that nobody ever sees or admires... they continue to do their work without a sign of vanity.

You will say, 'But the sun doesn't hide the fact that he is our source of light.' That is true. And it would be very difficult for him to do so, wouldn't it? In fact, we have the impression that he is happy to send his light out into space. It is as though he were saying, 'Look, I'm sending you light.' Yes, but behind the visible sun is another, invisible sun that we call the dark sun. It is from the dark sun that our sun continually receives the energies that it transforms and sends on to us in the form of light and heat. The dark sun never calls attention to itself, and it is this dark sun that all true spiritual Masters want to resemble. And this should be true of you, too. Whether anyone sees and appreciates you or not doesn't matter, but you must continue to do your work, for in this way you will become mighty and invulnerable and your life will be serene.

Everybody expects to get something from others – parents and children, employers and

employees, priests and their flock, teachers and
students. As for lovers... well, perhaps it is better
left unsaid. A boy gives a girl a little present and
expects a smile and some kisses in return; and if
she is a bit slow to make up her mind, he becomes
violent. We see examples of this every day.

But as for you, try to work to perfect yourselves. If you practise Karma-yoga you will be
on the path to perfection. Take every opportunity
to do all the good you can, whether by word, deed,
thought or feeling, and then leave the rest to time.
One day, even if you don't ask for anything, all the
good you have done will hunt you out and give you
your reward. And when that day comes, there will
be no way for you to hide or escape from it.

Chapter Seventeen


# LOVE WITHOUT ASKING TO BE LOVED
# IN RETURN

Love is a topic that will never be exhausted. Men and women can talk about it for ever without getting bored. It is like eating, drinking and breathing; man cannot live without loving, without talking and hearing about love. For thousands of years, love has been the subject of songs, paintings and books. In fact, we think that a novel, play or film that has no love-interest is dull. And yet, what do human beings really know about love? Isn't it the pain and suffering of love that they know best? And why is this? It is because, for most people, happiness consists not in loving but in being loved. Of course, they are willing to love a little as well, but they are convinced that it is more important to be loved. And if you doubt what I say, tell me this: why is it not enough for them to love? Why do they suffer so much when they find out that the person they love does not love them, or loves them less than they had hoped? They wait for love to come from others to make them happy. And if it doesn't come – or if it comes but doesn't last – they feel deprived. They have no faith in their own power to love, in the force of love within them. They need someone outside themselves to come and give them love.

Suppose you make a new friend and, for a time, you meet often and exchange ideas and warm, friendly glances and smiles. Then, one day, your friend is worried about something, he has problems and has less time to meet you or write to you or talk on the phone. You feel disappointed and unhappy because you think that he has abandoned you, and you start reproaching him: 'Why didn't you come and see me? Why didn't you ring me up?' and so on, until he is sick and tired of being badgered. Well, of course, it is normal that you should feel that you have lost something, but if you don't make up your mind to change your attitude you will never be free of suffering. If you want to regain your inner joy and peace, tell yourself that you must count only on your own love, and not expect it from others. As long as you expect and hope to be loved you will be dependent on others, and if others fail to love you or love you less than you would like – and they are perfectly within their rights in doing so – you will always be unhappy.

Life is such that we can never be sure of anything, either of events or of people. They will sometimes think of you, but they are far more likely to forget you. And this means that unless you anchor yourself to something stable within you, you will constantly be tossed about and driven off course. Yes, it is time to learn the true nature of things and understand what you have to do in order to be happy. And since you need love in order to be happy, since you feel that it is when you love that you flower and receive revelations, and since you long for your love to last for all eternity, love without asking to be loved. If those you love reciprocate your affection, so much the better; thank heaven for it, but don't count on it. If you can do this you will find happiness, for everything will depend on you alone; you can have what you want, as much as you want and where you want it. You will be all-powerful, independent, in charge of the situation.

The only thing you need to worry about is to manifest your love more perfectly, to make it purer and more luminous and selfless, less limited. This is the only condition that has to be fulfilled in order to be happy through love. Look at the sun, he doesn't wait to be loved; he is so radiant because he loves the whole world. He is free; he expects nothing from others.

For my part, I understood a long time ago that great grief and disappointment were in store for me if I relied on the love of the brothers and sisters of the Brotherhood. The poor things have so many problems and difficulties, so many commitments that hold them up, they don't have time to think of me. You will object, 'But they really do love you; if you could only hear what they say about you.' Yes, I know. They love me just as long as they haven't found someone else to love. When they find someone else they forget me. It is understandable... an old fellow with a beard who is always preaching about how they should respect the laws of God and exert themselves, and who gives them a good dressing down from time to time. Well, I can hardly blame them if they don't find that very appetizing. I have no illusions on the subject. This is why I am the first to apply my own advice. I tell myself that it is up to me to love them (but I don't show them that I love them, otherwise they would take advantage of it). And in this decision to love not only the brothers and sisters, but the whole of creation, the sun, the stars, the Lord himself and all the hierarchies of luminous creatures above... it is in this that I find happiness, a happiness that is stable, faithful and true. So why should you not do as I do?

Your love must grow in light and understanding. Don't limit yourselves to the dimension of feelings, because feelings are too personal. Understanding is also necessary in order to live the fullness of love. And it is when you make up your minds to love without waiting to be loved in return that you will truly be loved. Why? Because, if people feel illuminated and warmed in your presence, and at the same time feel completely free, how can they help loving you and finding you attractive?

And you will see for yourselves: as soon as you stop looking for love, it will pursue you. It will badger you, in fact. You will drive it out of the front door and it will sneak in again through the chimney. As soon as you stop searching for it, it will appear; but the more you search for it, the more it will evade you. It is like chasing your shadow; it keeps running away; you can never catch it. Yes, to look for love from others is like chasing after your own shadow. But if you stop chasing it, it will always be there, friendly and smiling, at your side. When you look for love from others, you focus on something extraneous, something outside yourselves, and your own love deserts you. This is just the way things are. Instead of looking for it from others, therefore, bring it out of yourselves and give it to them. In this way it will always be present within you and you will always be in control of the situation.

And now, if you don't want to believe me, you had better get your handkerchiefs ready. In any case, it is pretty harmless to have recourse to a handkerchief; there are worse things than that. Some people are not content with a handkerchief to mop up their tears; they prefer to have recourse to a dagger, a revolver or poison. I assure you, most tragedies are caused by love, by a wrong notion of love, by the kind of love that always wants something from others. But the love I am talking about, the love in which the Initiates dwell, rejuvenates and strengthens them and makes them tireless, luminous and beautiful. It is a love that gives eternal life and resuscitates and immortalizes.

Yes, when love is properly understood and manifested it possesses extraordinary power. Only love knows everything; only love is capable of remedying everything; the forces it can trigger and project are unimaginable.

It is said that God is love, but when one sees the human tragedies caused by love, one can see that there is still a great deal of work to be done, a very long upward path still to be travelled before the heights of divine love can be reached. But however great the effort required, it is well worth it, for the true magus, the only magus that is truly all-powerful, is love. You must invite it to dwell within you so that, wherever you go, like a great flame shining through the glass of a lamp, your love shines and radiates on all around you.

Chapter Eighteen


OUR ENEMIES ARE GOOD FOR US

Friends have always been considered one of the greatest boons in life. This is true; nothing is more precious than friendship. The only trouble is that we don't often look for true friends; we are more likely to ally ourselves with those who, we believe, will always approve and encourage us even when we are in the wrong. Do you know many people who accept complete sincerity on the part of their friends and don't expect them to approve of everything they do or say? Most people instantly feel betrayed and fly into a rage at the slightest criticism. We all know that if you want to win someone's good opinion, you have to praise and flatter and approve of him. This is why, with those who refuse to listen to the truth, on the one hand, and those who have discovered that it is not in their interest to tell it, on the other, we see so many people who spend their time deceiving or being deceived.

And they all imagine that, in doing so, they will be happy. Let me tell you that such behaviour will

never make them happy, because it is a manifestation of their lower nature and leads inevitably
to complications and disillusionment. He who truly
wants to evolve does not lie or try to deceive others;
above all, he accepts their comments or criticism.
In fact, if he is truly wise, he will understand that
it is good for him to have enemies. Why are enemies
good for one? Because they can help one to advance.
You will say, 'But we all have enemies; sometimes
too many, in fact.' Yes, you all have enemies, but
they don't do you any good, because you have never
learned to appreciate them. If you understood the
situation correctly, you would realize that it is they
that are your true friends. They are merciless; they
refuse to let you get away with anything; they spot
it immediately when you do something wrong. You
will say that they are not objective, that they often
exaggerate. That is true, but it doesn't matter; they
are like microscopes, and microscopes can
sometimes be very useful. Scientists use them every
day, because they enable them to see tiny details
that would otherwise go unnoticed.

If you sincerely want to make progress,
therefore, you must accept the idea that your
enemies can often be more useful to you in this
than your friends. It is they that oblige you to work
on yourself, to mend your ways and find solutions
to the problems they raise, and in this way, they
force you to become stronger and more intelligent.

It is important to understand the role of your enemies. If you don't understand this, you will detest them, they will make you suffer and you will keep trying to get rid of them or to revenge yourself on them. And what a waste of time and energy that will be! And yet there are not many human beings, even amongst the most highly intelligent, who are capable of accepting their enemies; most of them are too weak. They don't realize that, with the help of their friends and all their flattery, they become constantly weaker and more vulnerable. Well, all I can say is that, if there is one thing I have learned in life, it is to appreciate my enemies. Ah, yes; an enemy is really something... mine have rendered me invaluable services. It is a great pity that most people never appreciate them at their true worth.

We put up statues to those who are considered to be public benefactors. People who have saved their country or discovered a vaccine or been great poets or philosophers, etc., are placed on a pedestal. And this is only right and just; I am not saying that we should deprive them of their glory. But I still think that the most beautiful statues should be raised to our enemies, for it is they that are our true benefactors; it is thanks to them that we can become more vigilant, more intelligent and more patient. You think that I am not speaking seriously. Well, think what you like, but try, at least, to reflect about what I say when I tell you not to detest your enemies and not to run away from them, but to try to see how you can make use of them. If you do this you will make tremendous inner progress.

If you have a high ideal and a sincere desire to make progress, you will be given the knowledge and strength you need to use all the obstacles your enemies put in your path; they will be the stepping stones that will enable you to climb ever higher.

Chapter Nineteen

# THE GARDEN OF SOULS AND SPIRITS

Human beings can be compared to flowers or fruit – or even to vegetables. Every time you meet others, every time you talk to them and listen to them, you can enjoy their fragrance or taste their flavour. But is this what you actually do? No, you rarely pay attention to anything but their clothes or their jewellery, their faces, their legs or their hands; you never think of nourishing yourself on the life which is hidden under all that and which emanates from their heart, soul and spirit. And this is a great pity. Henceforth, try to be more attentive and learn to appreciate the human beings who are the bearers of this subtle life. Pause when you meet someone and say to yourself, 'He represents an aspect of the heavenly Father; she represents the divine Mother. Thank you, heavenly Father! Thank you, divine Mother! Thanks to these human "fruits and flowers" I can come closer to you and contemplate you today. Through their splendour, I can breathe your perfume and taste your sweetness.' And you will go on your way happy, because this fruit or flower will have brought you closer to heaven.

I know, of course, that some of you will be astonished that I should compare human beings to fruit, flowers and vegetables. But what is so astonishing about that? Poets are always comparing beautiful young girls or boys to roses, violets, lilies, jasmine or lotuses. And one of the favourite endearments of the French is, 'my little cabbage,' while someone who allows himself to be put upon is called a 'pear,' and someone who is stupid is called a 'gherkin.' Well, enough of this market-garden vocabulary. The important thing is to understand that this is an extremely effective method; if you learn to use it, not only will you avoid many mishaps and complications, but you will always be full of joy and inspiration.

How do men and women usually look at each other? What do they see? They see only the external appearance, the body or the clothes, and this proves that they do not possess true knowledge. It is exactly as though, looking at a car, you had eyes only for the bodywork and ignored the person behind the wheel, that is to say, the being that thinks, feels and acts. But it is precisely this being that you must learn to look for, that you must learn to see and feel in people. Always try to go further and deeper so as to discover the soul and spirit of those you meet, for it is there that you will discover riches and treasures, heaven itself.

It is simply a question of ridding yourselves of your habit of looking at things in a way that distorts and impoverishes life. All human beings have a body – that goes without saying – but that doesn't mean that you have to look at nothing but their stomachs or their intestines. What good will that do you? Of course, you will tell me that you are not interested in people's intestines, that what you look for in others is beauty and that you find that beauty in their eyes, their faces, hands and legs, etc. Well, there is nothing very wrong with that, but if you stop there and never go any further, you will be laying yourself open to disappointments, for you are confining yourself to details that are strictly material. If you want to feel continually happy and inspired, try to rejoice in the presence of all the flowers and fruit that surround you and enjoy their emanations, remembering that an invisible divinity is hidden in each one. Over and above a person's physical body are all those things that emanate from him on the subtle planes, and it is they that matter most.

As long as human beings continue to consider only each other's physical appearance they will never find the joy they seek. Someone who says, 'I need beauty and love,' should know that he will find them only when he learns to seek others in the fluidic world of emanations, radiations and vibrations. When you meet somebody wonderful and begin to love him and want to get to know him, instead of doing all you can to get close to him on the purely physical plane, learn to listen to the vibrations of his voice, to capture the light of his glance, to rejoice in the harmony of his gestures. In this way you will gradually build up a relationship with all that is most subtle and divine in him, and the sensations you experience will be beyond anything you have ever known or imagined. In the same way, you will also discover that people whom you may have been inclined to despise or ignore are, in reality, exceptional beings who can give you far more than many others who seem, outwardly, to be more interesting or attractive.

There is a whole new field of study for you here. Go ahead, do some experiments and analyse yourselves. Now that you know these truths, don't just ignore them and go on in the old way, repeating all the same unhappy experiences. For, I assure you, unless you change your point of view, your experiences will continue to be unhappy. Don't delude yourselves about this. It is no good believing in the impossible. You plunge into all kinds of adventures that can only end in grief and disenchantment, and you think, 'It was just bad luck; we could have been happy.' No, never!

Happiness and unhappiness are never a question of chance or luck. They depend on you. It is you yourselves who sow the seeds that will give you one or the other.

Chapter Twenty

# FUSION ON THE HIGHER PLANES

Nature has given every human being the instinctive desire to become one with another being whom he sees as the missing half of himself, the part that would make him whole; and until he finds this being he has a permanent sense of something lacking. Why is this? Because it is true that every individual needs that other half in order to be whole and capable of creating.

The question that arises, then, is why most people experience nothing but suffering and dissatisfaction even when they have found their other half. And the answer is that it is not enough to be united on the physical plane. If the union, the fusion of two beings, is to be perfect, it must take place on all three planes, that is to say, on the psychic plane (the heart and the mind) and on the spiritual plane (the soul and the spirit), as well. But what is the reality that we see all around us? A man and woman meet, find that they are more or less suited to each other and decide to live together, imagining that, in this way, they will fill their inner emptiness. Ah, what ignorance! They have no idea that the attraction that draws them together is not merely a superficial need that can easily be satisfied; it is the manifestation of a cosmic phenomenon that concerns, first and foremost, their soul and spirit. This is why the fusion of a man and woman must be accomplished first of all on a higher plane, in the divine world, in the world of light. Only when this union exists, can it take place on the physical plane as well. Then, and only then, will they know wholeness and fulfilment and that fulfilment will produce creations of untold beauty.

From what I have been saying, you will understand why the Initiates teach that we must attune ourselves to heaven, to the divine world for, without this link with heaven, all our human relationships are bound to fail in the long run. To attune oneself and be in harmony with heaven is to vibrate on the same wavelength; that is to say, to adapt and conform and be receptive. There is no other way to receive anything from heaven. Heaven never forces itself on someone who is unreceptive; it never behaves like those brutes who overpower a woman and take her by force. Harmony can only exist if the two wills seek the same goal. If the masculine, emissive principle tries to impose its will and the receptive feminine principle resists, there can be no question of harmony. Harmony implies agreement, accord between at least two principles or elements.

And since we all possess both the masculine and feminine principles within ourselves, to achieve harmony with heaven means, first of all, that we have to work to accomplish the necessary inner purification and elevation and synchronize our vibrations with those of the divine world (this is the work of the masculine principle). Then, in a climate of inner peace and silence, we open ourselves to heaven and allow it to form its reflection within us and pour into us all its effluvia, all its radiance, all the seeds of life that are destined to grow and burgeon in our hearts and souls (and this is the work of the feminine principle).

In our spiritual work, therefore, we make use of the two principles, the active masculine principle that enables us to reach up to the divine world, and the receptive feminine principle that transforms us into a vessel awaiting the outpouring of divine blessings. This is what the work of harmonization really means, therefore: a work with the two principles. Before the receptive principle can achieve union with heaven, the active principle must work to achieve order and purity. True creation is possible only if this condition is satisfied.

As you can see, the spiritual polarity of a human being can be alternately feminine and masculine. This means that we are always richer and more complete on the spiritual plane, for on

the physical plane we always have many
shortcomings and imperfections. And just as a
woman bears in her womb the child whose seed
has been given to her on the physical plane by a
man, so, on the spiritual plane, the soul conceives
and gives birth to children whose seed is given
by the spirit. And now, if you want to be happy, the
most important thing for you to understand is this:
before uniting yourself physically with a man or a
woman, you must achieve union on the higher
plane, on the level of your soul and spirit. The act
that you accomplish on the physical plane with a
physical being is no more than a dim reflection
of the cosmic act of fusion between the spiritual
principle within you and the principle of God
himself, your spirit. And since this act is no more
than a reflection, it will always end in
disillusionment if you have not first achieved union
on the higher plane.

You will ask, 'Does this mean that we must
wait until we have achieved this spiritual fusion
before we can be united to a man or woman?' No;
I am not saying that you must necessarily wait. I
am saying – because this is the reality – that there
can be no true and lasting union between a man
and a woman on the physical plane if they are not
united, first of all, on the spiritual plane. But as far
as each one of you is concerned, I can only say that
you must do what you can.

On the physical plane, a man is always a man and a woman is always a woman (the rare exceptions don't concern us here). But on the spiritual plane, every human being is both man and woman; in his soul he is a woman and in his spirit he is a man. On the spiritual plane, therefore, human beings are androgynous. In fact, one aspect of this reality is reflected in our physical bodies, in the way our mouths are made: the tongue (the masculine principle) collaborates with the two lips (the feminine principle) to produce words, speech.

An Initiate who understands the immense wisdom that cosmic intelligence has hidden in the mouth, strives every day, through his meditations, to penetrate and fertilize the infinite light that we call the universal soul by projecting into it his thought and will. And once he has achieved this, he abandons himself in turn to the action of the universal spirit, opening his soul to receive the living seeds that are destined to germinate and blossom into inspiration and joy.

The desire to love and be loved, the desire to create, is perfectly legitimate, and even when it manifests itself on the physical plane, its origin and source is on a higher level. This is why you must prepare yourselves so that the union on the physical plane may take place in conditions that are pure and sacred. Instead of being in a hurry to find someone with whom, once physical union has been consummated, you run the risk of feeling more alone and unhappy than ever, you should try to unite yourself to the universal soul, if you are a man, and to the cosmic spirit, if you are a woman. So many people come and complain to me: 'I have never found the man – or woman – with whom I would want to share my life.' And all I can say is, 'It's just as well!' because, judging from the way they are going about it, they would not be together for long.

Yes, a heart seeks and finds another heart, but then the intellect comes between them and separates them. And this will always be the case if you remain on the level of the heart and the intellect. It is only on the level of the soul and spirit that there can be no divorce, for the soul and spirit work together, just as the tongue and lips work together in the mouth to create speech. So, any of you who have still not met the man or woman of your life must not be distressed, for nothing is lost. Take advantage of this time of waiting to prepare yourselves divinely.

Those who truly know how to seek will find; and if it is not on the physical plane, it will be on the spiritual plane. Jesus said, 'Seek and you will find.' Yes, you will find, but only if you seek in the world above. Jesus did not tell us to seek in the dust and mud underfoot. Of course, you can always seek down there, if you want to, but then you will have no reason to be surprised by what you find. In any case, if you really want to find true love, you must realize that you will find it only in the world above. Those who have sought it there sincerely and honestly have always found it. For all that exists on the physical plane exists also on the subtle planes, and if you manage to reach that level, you will continue to eat and love and work, but the dimensions of these activities will be much vaster, and the joys you experience will never be followed by the bitter pangs of disenchantment.

Those who have attained union with the divine principle within them, with the cosmic spirit or the universal soul, truly know the fullness of love, and they can continue to live in that fullness on the physical plane as long as they maintain their union on the higher plane. In this case, everything becomes divine, for they have the power to purify, illuminate and transform matter. But those who are neither enlightened nor in control of themselves, those whose behaviour is ruled by instinct and passion, are incapable of transforming matter. This is why they are obliged to endure the alternation of love and hatred, joy and grief. After fulfilment and ecstasy comes the plunge into emptiness and grief.

Of course, it is perfectly true that love can be a source of tremendous joy to everyone, even if they have never practised any spiritual discipline.

Yes, but the trouble is that these joys are always
followed by disenchantment, and it is this that men
and women are so reluctant to believe. Once they
have found a little happiness, they think that it is
going to last for ever. But this is not so; it cannot
last. If they wanted their happiness to last, they
should have looked for it on a very high level, in
a region that is not subject to change. Here below,
everything is unstable and constantly subject to
change; it is essential to understand this and to
know that what you mistake for gold soon tarnishes
and turns into lead. If your love is to be of pure
gold, it must contain divine elements. I assure you,
if you are so naïve as to think otherwise, your life
will inevitably be a succession of disappointments.

It is not enough to say, 'I love him' or 'I love
her,' and throw yourself headlong into the adventure
of love. You must prepare yourselves to live that
adventure in its most exalted dimension; only when
you are capable of this will your love not only make
you happy, but by its vibrations and emanations it
will trigger all kinds of beneficial forces and
contribute to the good of the whole world... even
to the coming of the kingdom of God.

Are you beginning to understand now that
something much more profound and much vaster
than anything you had ever imagined is involved?
But who can be bothered to study all the etheric
phenomena produced by the forces of love? People

fall in love, kiss and sleep together, and never wonder what is actually happening within them. You will say, 'But what is there to study? You don't need to study in order to understand what is happening when you fall in love. You love, that's all, and you want to express and receive an expression of that love. You don't need or expect anything else.' Ah, but this is where you are wrong.

For thousands of years, human beings ate and slept and brought children into the world without knowing how any of these processes worked until, one day, they felt the need to understand what was involved in digestion, sleep, conception, gestation and so on. And now that they know, they are in a position to nourish themselves better, to sleep better and to ensure better conditions for bringing children into the world. In the same way, there is still a great deal to be learned about love, about the effects it can have on the human psyche, about the forces and currents it sets in motion on the subtle planes and about the regions in which it circulates in man and in the cosmos. There is a whole science here that is waiting to be discovered by human beings.

And now I want to add something very important. When, in his meditations, an Initiate succeeds in reaching the sublime regions of divine love, he receives from these regions etheric particles of the utmost purity. And these particles work their way down onto the physical plane and are absorbed by all the cells of his physical body. The sensation of completion and fulfilment he experiences is such, then, that he needs nothing else. Physical desire has no longer the power to torment him, for heaven itself has truly taken possession not only of his heart and soul but even of his physical organs. But here, too, it is important to be vigilant and not allow oneself any illusions. Many people, even saints and mystics, have only succeeded in unleashing their own unbridled passions through their meditations. Yes, simply because they had not worked sufficiently to achieve self-mastery and purity. For, although everyone can make an effort to make his love more spiritual, it is not given to everyone to experience true mystical ecstasy.

This work represents the very highest form of alchemy. Those who have not worked to purify themselves sufficiently to open the etheric channels of their subtle bodies find these channels blocked, and, when this happens, the divine energies remain on the higher planes; they cannot work their way down. This explains why such people live in a state of burning frustration as though they were being consumed by flames.

In the Emerald Tablet, Hermes Trismegistus says, 'With great sagacity it doth ascend gently from earth to heaven. Again it doth descend to earth, and uniteth in itself the force from things superior and things inferior;' and, 'This is the strength of all strengths for it overcometh every subtle thing and doth penetrate every solid substance.' This 'strength of all strengths' which Hermes Trismegistus calls Telesma, is the force of love, and an Initiate must reach up and take possession of this force in its subtle state and then bring it down into the depths of his own being so that all his cells may be steeped in it. It is not enough for him to rise to where he can touch and grasp this divine energy, he must also be capable of drawing it downwards into his own being, otherwise he will be more and more unhappy and frustrated. Many biographies of the saints and mystics give some idea of the ravages a mistaken notion of mystical love can cause in a human being. And then, of course, there are always plenty of so-called sensible, reasonable people who use these cases as an argument to support their claim that it is dangerous to dedicate oneself to God and to seek the fulfilment of love in him.

No, there is no danger for those who are enlightened. Those who are enlightened know that they will never find God's love if they have not started by ridding themselves of all the thoughts and sentiments whose vibrations are not in harmony with this cosmic force. As long as this work of purification is not done, whatever efforts they may make to attain this force they will still not be able to draw it into themselves, for divine energy will never be poured into a vessel, a receptacle, that is not fit to receive it.

Our teaching is the teaching of love. We keep coming back to the question of love, constantly seeking to explain and throw more light onto it, for everything depends on love; all strength, balance, peace and happiness depend on love. You must come to feel that love is there within your reach, that it is within you and that you have absolutely no reason to feel poor and lonely. If you feel poor and lonely, it is because you have not managed to free yourself from the physical plane. As soon as you attain the subtler planes – especially when you attain the regions of the soul and the spirit – it is no longer possible to feel abandoned, for the universal soul and the universal spirit are always there, always in and around you, and you can communicate with them whenever you wish. Whereas, can you ever be sure that a man or a woman, however wonderful, will not be obliged to think of other things and abandon you?

Believe me, therefore, even if you have found the most magnificent being on earth, don't stop there. Thank heaven for allowing you to find such a marvellous being, but remember that love will bring you happiness only if you know how to find it in the realms of the soul and the spirit.

Chapter Twenty-One


# WE ARE THE ARTISANS OF
# OUR OWN FUTURE

# I

Our present is the result of our past. This is why we have practically no power over it; it is the consequence, the logical outcome of the past. The thoughts, feelings and desires that we nourished in our previous incarnations have set in motion forces and powers of the same nature in the universe, and it is they that determine our strengths and weaknesses and the events that affect us today. You will ask, 'But how can they determine these things?' Well, first of all, you must realize that thousands of years before our contemporaries invented computers cosmic intelligence had perfected its own recording techniques. All the data concerning the actions of human beings, even down to the least little detail of their private lives, are fed into the cosmic computer, and the infallible, implacable result appears on its screen. There is no need for a God, fate, a judge – or whatever else you call it – to wrack its brains to decide what each man or woman deserves in the way of punishment or reward. There is this cosmic machine which decides it automatically.

This is why it is virtually impossible in our present incarnation to change what has been determined by our past. The only thing that it is in our power to do is to prepare the future. Yes, and this is something that is far from clear for most people. They argue endlessly about whether man is free or not; some say that he is, others that he is not, but in fact, they put the question the wrong way. Freedom is not a condition that is given or withheld once and for all. As far as our present is concerned, our freedom is very limited, because the present is the consequence of a past which cannot be revised or changed. We can only endure and digest the past. But it is in respect to our future that we are free; we have the possibility of creating whatever kind of future we want.

This is an extremely important truth, and we need to know it in order to understand the direction our work should take. Otherwise, what happens? If we don't know that we can improve the situation for the future, we simply endure the present and slip into ways that are more and more deplorable, with the result that, in the next incarnation, we shall have even less freedom and be even more thoroughly enslaved.

You can start immediately, today, to prepare your future. By means of your wishes, your thoughts, your imagination, you can choose an orientation and ask for the best qualities and the best conditions, so that you may manifest yourself, one day, as beings of peace, goodness and light. For this is an absolute truth: you will return to this earth, one day, and what you are and what happens to you then, will depend entirely on you and on how you have prepared your future incarnation. An understanding of this truth is fundamental to your destiny.

The great mistake of many spiritual people is to believe that in choosing the path of goodness and light their lives will immediately be transformed. Inwardly, perhaps, they may be transformed, but they can gain nothing by deluding themselves; this incarnation will involve many payments, much suffering, much settling of accounts, for they still have past debts to pay off. They will be free only when they have honestly settled all their debts. And this applies to all of you, too: you will be free only when you have paid your debts. This is why, when you encounter difficulties and trials, instead of rebelling against them or giving way to despair, you should understand that they are necessary and try to put up with them. If you refuse to accept them you will only break even more laws, and in your next incarnation your debts will be all the heavier and you will have to suffer all the more.

Let nothing stop you from continuing to build your future; if you persevere, your trials will be no more than passing storms and you will soar above them. Yes, if human beings feel so defeated by their trials it is because they cannot see the light of the future ahead of them; the horizon is hidden by a dark cloud. But it is hidden because they themselves have hidden it; all they have to do is open a window and they will see the sun.

Many of you will tell me, of course, that they already work for the future, for their own and their children's future. Yes, I know; they put money in the bank, they buy shares on the stock-market and they take out life insurance… and they think they are working for the future. But for heaven's sake, what do they mean by the future? The future is far more than the thirty, forty or fifty years that still remain of their life on earth, far more even than the duration of their children's and grand-children's lives. The future, the true future I am talking about, consists in your future incarnations, and you must prepare for it by putting certain qualities and virtues into practice.

Far too many people – even some of you – are mesmerised by the idea of amassing material possessions for themselves and their children. It is normal to ensure that one's family has what it needs to live on, but why waste all your time and energy running after so many other things that are not really necessary? Life is so short! How many years will you have in which to enjoy all those possessions? Not only will you be unable to take them with you into the next world, but when you get there, everything will disappear so swiftly that you will not even remember that you once possessed a palace or that you were chairman of the board, Cabinet minister or president.

The future for which human beings claim to work is so near that it will very soon be the present, a present that will have gone in a flash. In other words, they are working in a vacuum, they are working for the wind. Yes, the events of this life, even those that are still to come, belong in reality to the present. The future is something else; you still don't know what it really is. The future I am talking about does not belong to the same dimension as past and present; it is eternity, infinity, and it is this future that we have the power to create. We have no power to wipe out the past or to change the present, but we have the power to create the future. God gave us this power. By the means of thought, desire, will-power, we can do everything. But as long as we do not know nothing that this power exists, we can never do much to improve our situation; in fact, we shall often succeed in making things worse.

I know that some of those who are listening to what I say will be thinking, 'For heaven's sake! Has he been living on another planet? Doesn't he know how complicated life is? He seems to have no idea of all the difficulties, of all the financial problems and ill-health we have to contend with. And he talks about a future of splendour and perfection. He's really up in the clouds. How can he hope to convince us with such an unrealistic philosophy?' Let me tell you that I know far better than you those so-called realities of life: privation, adversity, hostility, and so on; but I have always refused to dwell on these realities, for I know that they represent only one, insignificant aspect of the true reality.

Believe me, the difficulties I have to contend with are just as bad as yours. Worse, in fact. The only difference is that I have a philosophy of life capable of remedying this harsh, prosaic reality in which we are all immersed. And you, instead of rejecting this philosophy of the Initiates on the pretext that it is unrealistic, why don't you make the effort to adopt it, knowing that it can help you to overcome and solve all your problems? However great the sufferings imposed on you, however weak or wretched you are, tell yourselves that you must never surrender. All those things are temporary, and conditions will soon begin to improve.

If there is so much disorder and chaos in the lives of individuals and society today, it is because human beings have abandoned the true philosophy and adopted a pernicious philosophy that teaches that man is purely material and that his life is ruled by chance. Even religion, whose mission it was to hold aloft the torch of the spirit, has become materialized. And when man no longer has the life of the spirit to sustain him he is like a tree cut off from its roots, and he wastes away. Then the door lies open to every form of physical and psychic ill, and it is no good looking to medical science for a cure, for it can offer only temporary relief. If you yourself open the door to evil you cannot expect to conquer it. What is the good of fighting it, if, at the same time, you continue to nourish it?

The only solution is to replace this materialistic philosophy by the philosophy of the spirit bequeathed to us by the Initiates of the past. All those who have truly accepted and lived by that philosophy have manifested themselves as beings of balance, peace and light, so why don't you turn back to it? You will say, 'But that already is our philosophy. We already live by that philosophy.' That is what you believe, but analyse yourselves and you will see that you are still subjugated by all kinds of preoccupations that have nothing spiritual about them. True, your philosophy includes a few bits and pieces that you have accepted from the Initiates, because they give you a clear conscience, but you mix them up with all kinds of futile details about the latest exploits of such and such a politician, or the latest gems fallen from the lips or the pen of this artist or that intellectual. I am not

saying that you should take absolutely no interest
in these things, but there are other things that are
so much more important. Yes, truly! It is far more
important to interest yourselves in the creatures
that inhabit the luminous regions of space and in
the work they are doing; it is far more important
to interest yourselves in the laws that govern the
future of mankind, For this is where our life really
lies. It does not lie in the things that the newspapers,
radio and television talk about. It lies in that
essential, eternal world in which we are destined,
one day, to participate.

Be on your guard, therefore; you are still far too
inclined to mix up spirituality and materialism. The
two philosophies wander about and get tangled up
inside you and you must get them sorted out. As
Hermes Trismegistus says, you must 'separate the
subtle from the gross with great diligence.' This
alchemical precept is valid on every plane, and
particularly on the plane of thought. It is on the plane
of thought that you must separate this materialistic
philosophy that is so prejudicial to your
development from the philosophy of the Initiates,
the philosophy that can give you the impetus you
need to grow and develop in the divine world.

Remember to devote a few minutes every day
to creating your future, in the knowledge that you
have the same power over that future as God
himself. There is not much you can do about the

present, that is true, but you are all-powerful where the future is concerned, for you are all sons and daughters of God and the spark that lives within you desires nothing more than to return to the primordial fire from which it came.

You will object, 'But we are all so handicapped; so wretched. What is the use of imagining a wonderful future?' Well, let me tell you that this argument only shows that your reasoning is faulty. It is not those who are already happy and well-off but those who are unhappy who need to imagine and wish for something better; and their wishing will be a hundred times more powerful than that of the rich. So if you feel so impoverished, now is the time to apply your thoughts to the creation of a future of wealth and splendour.

What is your reaction when you know that you are about to inherit a fortune or go on a long journey? You look forward with delight to all the things you will do with that fortune, to all that you expect to discover and enjoy on your journey. Why can't you react in the same way when it comes to something that is so much more important than money or a journey: your divine future? To be sure, it is a question of imagination, but imagination is not unproductive. The thoughts and sentiments generated by the imaginative representation of this divine future actually influence and transform your destiny.

## II

What do you need in life? Fresh air, water, a little bread... and a lot of hope. Yes, and it is at sunrise every morning that you can go hunting for hope, as you would hunt for game, for it is at sunrise that hope is most abundant; this is the best time to catch it. It is the sun that gives us hope. The sun says, 'Look at me. Has any misfortune ever overwhelmed me? I am always here, always luminous and unchanging. Cling to me and you will become like me. For it is I who distribute the quintessence of hope; I who am your future.'

Where do you expect to find your future? Your future is there. It is the sun. One day you will be like the sun; even the earth will become a sun. The earth is a fruit which is in the process of ripening; at the moment it is still hard and sour and bitter, and I don't advise you to taste it. But the sun looks at it and caresses it with patience and love so as to ripen it, and one day, millions of years hence, it will be like its father, the sun.

The earth is a child of the sun; it came from the womb of the sun. It is the sun that launched it into being, and he continues to nourish and educate it so that it may become wise and reasonable and learn to give as he gives. So far, the earth is more accustomed to taking than to giving. To be sure, it gives a little vegetation, a few fruits, but it is still a long way from being capable of giving with the generosity of the sun. This means that it must continue to learn, continue to look at the sun and listen to what he tells it: 'You must learn to give and radiate as I do; you must learn to smile and not be so wrapped up in yourself.' And the earth listens to what the sun says and tries, every day, to become a little more like him.

You will say, 'Yes, but is the sun speaking about us as well?' Indeed he is. Human beings and the earth have the same origin and the same destiny. Each human being is a tiny earth, and each one of these earths must become like the sun. This is the future that is in store for mankind. Many of you will say, 'Oh, we never imagined anything of the kind.' Naturally, when a man's mind is busy with the thought of cigarettes, wine, money, mistresses or cars, he cannot hear the sun talking about his luminous future.

All the great Masters and Initiates teach that man is a spirit, a flame that sprang, like the earth itself, from the bosom of the Almighty. He has a long journey to make, and he too can easily lose his light and warmth and become cold and inert along the way. But he is predestined to return to the regions from which he came; one day, after a very long time and many, many incarnations, just as the earth will become like the sun, so will man return to the bosom of his heavenly Father. The laws and correspondences are the same in both cases.

As you see, the Initiates have left us keys that enable us to decipher all that has been created by God. So, you must never forget this: your future is to resemble God himself. If you forget this wisdom, this light, you need not be surprised when you meet with all kinds of disappointments, bitterness and despair. And when this happens, of course, you will keep the doctors busy. So many men and women are on the brink of the abyss, and doctors have all sorts of scientific terms for their condition: 'depression,' 'neurosis,' 'melancholia,' etc.. But the fact is that they are all suffering from the same sickness: they have forgotten the true nature of man, his divine essence and his ultimate destination in the bosom of the eternal Lord. This is why you must cling to the sun and think about your luminous future, every day.

Human beings often wonder what life on earth will be like in ten, fifty, a hundred years from now. The question is important, to be sure, but the essential thing to know is that, one day, human beings will shine with the brilliance of the sun, that their presence will perfume the air, that they will smell the fragrance of each other's souls and that symphonies will be heard wherever they go, for all their cells will sing. Every day, if only for a few minutes at a time, picture this magnificent future to yourselves and you will immediately feel your courage and cheerfulness restored. This is what it means to become a new being. Wherever you go these days, you hear the word 'new:' a new philosophy, a new science, a new era, a new type of human being. But how can you imagine that you are a new man if you are always tense, morose and lustreless?

You attend the sunrise in order to receive the fruit of hope. Yes, how often, thanks to its light, warmth and life, the sun has nourished you and quenched your thirst with hope. And what a pity that you have so often abandoned that hope and put despair in its place. If you had not abandoned it, if you had not given way so often to doubt and hesitation, you would have made much more progress. Why don't you cultivate thoughts that nourish your spirit? If you make no attempt to free yourselves from the sad reality that is oppressing you, you will really end by being suffocated. You must change something, if only inwardly, by telling yourself, 'None of this will last. I am a son of God, a daughter of God, and God is preparing a future of beauty, light and splendour for me.'

You still do not know what hope really is. Hope is a wisdom that knows how to use the past and the present in order to shape the future. Hope is the ability to live a magnificent reality that has not yet come about on the physical plane. Hope is a foretaste of perfection. Thanks to hope, you can eat and drink a happiness which you do not yet possess but which is a reality, true reality. For true reality is not on the physical plane; it is in the divine world. The true reality is that you are heirs to heaven and earth. Your inheritance is there but, as you are still too young, you cannot yet take possession of it.

You are princes and princesses, and a kingdom awaits you. Should you despair and lose courage just because you still have to wait a little while? 'That's all very well,' you will say, 'But in the meantime my life is miserable; I wear myself out working; nobody shows me any respect; in fact, I am constantly being insulted.' True, but all that is necessary. This apprenticeship that the King, your Father, is asking you to serve, is his way of educating you. Yes, for education exists in the kingdom of God also. In fact, true education is precisely this: the Lord says, 'When this child comes into his kingdom, he will have immense power over millions of creatures, and what will happen if he has never learned to be kind, patient and courageous? He will be a cruel, cowardly, lazy despot, giving in to every passing whim and treating everybody as though they were all his servants. For this reason I shall let him take possession of his kingdom only when he has proved that he will never abuse his power or his wealth. Not before.'

So, you can hope and look forward to every good thing but, in the meantime, work. Hope shapes and realizes the future on the subtle planes, for it is a magical force.

And now, let me assure you that I know your situation well. If I give you methods of this kind, it is not in order to make fun of you; it is in order to be useful to you, in order to help you to understand where true happiness lies. Accept these methods, therefore, and try them out for yourselves. You are so fascinated and deceived by the gross, material reality that surrounds you that you cannot see the other, subtler reality that is also there waiting for you. But, of course, you must do as you please. I can only tell you what is best for you, and it is up to you to make your own decisions.

Genesis tells us that man was created in the image of God, but very few people take this idea seriously when the question of their sublime future is being discussed. And yet, if you admit that man was created in the image of God, you must be logical and accept the consequences of that truth. And one of these consequences is precisely this: that a sublime, divine future awaits all human beings. We have no right to suppress half of this truth, for if we do so, what kind of future could we envisage for God's image?

**World Wide - Editor-Distributor**
**Editions PROSVETA S.A. - B.P. 12 - F- 83601 Fréjus Cedex (France)**
Tel. (00 33) 04 94 40 82 41 - Fax (00 33) 04 94 40 80 05
Web: **www.prosveta.com**
e-mail: **international@prosveta.com**

**Distributors**

**AUSTRALASIA**
**Australia - New Zealand - Hong Kong - Taïwan - Singapour**
SURYOMA LTD - P.O. Box 2218 – Bowral – N.S.W. 2576
e-mail: info@suryoma.com – Tel. (61) 2 4872 3999 – fax (61) 2 4872 4022

**AUSTRIA**
HARMONIEQUELL VERSAND – A- 5302 Henndorf am Wallersee, Hof 37
Tel. / fax (43) 6214 7413 – e-mail: info@prosveta.at

**BELGIUM & LUXEMBOURG**
PROSVETA BENELUX  – Liersesteenweg 154 B-2547 Lint
Tel (32) 3/455 41 75 – Fax 3/454 24 25 – e-mail: prosveta@skynet.be
N.V. MAKLU Somersstraat 13-15 – B-2000 Antwerpen
Tel. (32) 3/231 29 00 – Fax 3/233 26 59
VANDER S.A. – Av. des Volontaires 321 – B-1150 Bruxelles
Tel. (32) 27 62 98 04 –  Fax 27 62 06 62

**BULGARIA**
SVETOGLED – Bd Saborny 16 A, appt 11 – 9000 Varna
e-mail: svetgled@revolta.com – Tel/Fax: (359) 52 23 98 02

**CANADA**
PROSVETA Inc. – 3950, Albert Mines – North Hatley (Qc), J0B 2C0
Tel. (819) 564-8212 – Fax. (819) 564-1823
in Canada, call toll free: 1-800-854-8212
e-mail: prosveta@prosveta-canada.com / www.prosveta-canada.com

**COLUMBIA**
PROSVETA – Calle 146 # 25-28 Aptp 404 Int.2 – Bogotá
e-mail: kalagiya@tutopia.com

**CYPRUS**
THE SOLAR CIVILISATION BOOKSHOP – BOOKBINDING
73 D Kallipoleos Avenue - Lycavitos - P. O. Box 24947, 1355 – Nicosia
Tel / Fax 00357-2-377503

**CZECH REPUBLIC**
PROSVETA – Ant. Sovy 18, –České Budejovice 370 05
Tel / Fax: (420) 38-53 00 227 – e-mail: prosveta@iol.cz

**GERMANY**
PROSVETA Deutschland – Postfach 16 52 – 78616 Rottweil
Tel. (49) 741-46551 – Fax. (49) 741-46552 – e-mail: prosveta.de@t-online.de
EDIS GmbH, Mühlweg 2 – 82054 Sauerlach
Tel. (49) 8104-6677-0 – Fax.(49) 8104-6677-99

**GREAT BRITAIN – IRELAND**
PROSVETA – The Doves Nest, Duddleswell Uckfield, – East Sussex TN 22 3JJ
Tel. (44) (01825) 712988 - Fax (44) (01825) 713386
e-mail: prosveta@pavilion.co.uk

**GREECE**
PROSVETA – J. Vamvacas
Moutsopoulou 103 – 18541 Piraeus

**HAITI**
PROSVETA – DÉPÔT – B.P. 115, Jacmel, Haiti (W.I.)
Tel./ Fax (509) 288-3319
e-mail: uwbhaiti@citeweb.net

**HOLLAND**
STICHTING PROSVETA NEDERLAND
Zeestraat 50 – 2042 LC Zandvoort – e-mail: prosveta@worldonline.nl
**ISRAEL**
Zohar, P. B. 1046, Netanya 42110
e-mail: zohar@wanadoo.fr
**ITALY**
PROSVETA Coop. – Casella Postale – 06060 Moiano (PG)
Tel. (39) 075-8358    orden - prosnor@online.no
**PORTUGAL & BRAZIL**
EDIÇÕES PROSVETA – Rua Passos Manuel, n° 20 – 3e E, P 1150 – Lisboa
Tel. (351) (21) 354 07 64
PUBLICAÇÕES EUROPA-AMERICA Ltd
Est Lisboa-Sintra KM 14 – 2726 Mem Martins Codex
e-mail : prosvetapt@hotmail.com
**ROMANIA**
ANTAR – Str. N. Constantinescu 10  - Bloc 16A - sc A - Apt. 9,
Sector 1 – 71253 Bucarest
Tel. (40) 1 679 52 48 - Tel./ Fax (40) 1 231 37 19
e-mail : antared@pcnet.ro
**RUSSIA**
EDITIONS PROSVETA
Riazanski Prospekt 8a, office 407 – 109428 Moscou
Tel / Fax (7095) 232 08 79 – e-mail : prosveta@online.ru
**SPAIN**
ASOCIACIÓN PROSVETA ESPAÑOLA – C/ Ausias March n° 23 Ático
SP-08010 Barcelona – Tel (34) (3) 412 31 85 - Fax (34) (3) 302 13 72
aprosveta@prosveta.es
**SWITZERLAND**
PROSVETA Société Coopérative – CH - 1808 Les Monts-de-Corsier
Tel. (41) 21 921 92 18 – Fax. (41) 21 922 92 04
e-mail: prosveta@swissonline.ch
**UNITED STATES**
PROSVETA U.S.A. – P.O. Box 1176 – New Smyrna Beach, FL.32170-1176
Tel / Fax (386) 428-1465
e-mail: sales@prosveta-usa.com – web page: www.prosveta-usa.com
**VENEZUELA**
PROSVETA VENEZUELA C. A. – Calle Madrid
Quinta Monteserino – D. F. Las Mercedes – Caracas
Tel. (58) 0414 22 36 748 – e-mail : miguelclavijo@hotmail.com

Achevé d'imprimer en décembre 2001
sur les presses de l'Imprimerie HEMISUD
83160 – La Valette-du-Var